A NOTE TO REA

The dust storms of the 1930s are a part of ... many of us cannot imagine. Sometimes they were six hundred miles wide and lasted for ten hours. Parts of Texas, Colorado, Oklahoma, and Kansas were in the dust bowl. The storms in *Rosa Takes a Chance* are based on the dates of storms that actually happened in Rosa's corner of Texas. "Black Sunday" is one of the most famous. After this storm, many families across the Great Plains decided to look for a better life by moving west, just like the families Rosa knew.

SISTERS IN TIME

Rosa
Takes a Chance

MEXICAN IMMIGRANTS IN
THE DUST BOWL YEARS

SUSAN MARTINS MILLER

BARBOUR
PUBLISHING

Rosa
Takes a Chance

ISBN 1-59789-065-0

Cover design by Lookout Design Group, Inc.

Published by Barbour Publishing, Inc., P.O. Box 719, Uhrichsville, Ohio 44683
www.barbourbooks.com

Our mission is to publish and distribute inspirational products offering exceptional value and biblical encouragement to the masses.

 Member of the
Evangelical Christian
Publishers Association

Printed in the United States of America.

5 4 3 2 1

CONTENTS

EXPLANATION OF TERMS

Spanish words used in the text:

El Nacimiento	The Nativity; representation of where Jesus was born
Feliz Navidad	Merry Christmas
Hermana	Sister
Hermano	Brother
Hija ("mi hija")	Daughter ("my daughter")
Hijos	Sons
Hombre	Man
La maestra	The teacher
Las Posadas	A nine-day Christmas festivity
Mamá	Mama, Mother
Papá	Papa, Father
Rosita	Nickname for Rosa
San José	Joseph (Jesus' earthly father)
Santa Biblia	Holy Bible
Señor	Mr.
Señora	Mrs.
Señorita	Miss
Tía	Aunt
Tío	Uncle
Virgen Maria	Virgin Mary (Jesus' mother)

CHAPTER 1

Words in the Dirt

"If I grow up to be a teacher, I will be a real teacher." Rosa Sanchez spoke aloud, but no one listened. She sat alone on the cement steps outside her school while other children played. "I will not be a teacher like *Señora* Gonzalez. We call her *la maestra*, the teacher, but she does not teach us. She only wants us to play."

"Rosa!" Maria called to her friend. "Come jump rope with us."

Maria spoke in Spanish, but Rosa answered her in English.

"No thanks," Rosa said. "I do not want to jump rope. I want to read."

"Why?" Maria asked in Spanish. "It's a nice day to play."

"Speak English," Rosa insisted.

"I like Spanish," Maria answered. She scampered back to the jump-rope line.

"I like Spanish, too," Rosa told herself. "But my family is not in Mexico any longer. If I want to go to a real school, I must learn better English."

At home, Rosa's family spoke Spanish. They had all learned a few English words. But many people in Texas spoke Spanish, so the Sanchez family did not speak English very often. They joked in Spanish. They sang in Spanish. They told stories of Mexico in Spanish. Sometimes they prayed in Spanish. The *Santa Biblia*,

9

the Holy Bible, that *Papá* kept on the shelf in the big room was in Spanish. Their friends were other Mexican families who also spoke Spanish. Rosa did not have many opportunities to speak English.

Rosa's parents had moved from Mexico to Texas with three little boys before Rosa was born. *Mamá*'s brother, José, came with them. Rosa was soon born, and ten years passed. Now *Tío* José had a wife, *Tía* Natalia. Tío and Tía had a new baby, little Isabella. They all lived together in Dalhart, in the northwest corner of Texas. The men worked in the pastures of a large cattle ranch. They branded the cattle, checked to be sure the animals were healthy, drove them to new pastures when they needed fresh grass to graze, and got them ready to sell at the cattle auction in town. Rosa's brothers helped Papá and Tío José make sure the cows had food and were safe.

The cows belonged to the man who owned the ranch. Papá and Tío got part of the profit from selling the cattle. The owner also gave the Sanchez family a small house to live in so they could work for him. Nine people lived in six rooms. It was crowded, but they were happy. Downstairs, the house had a kitchen and a big room. Rosa's brothers slept on the porch, which had walls and big windows. Upstairs, the house had three bedrooms. Mamá and Papá slept in one room. Tío and Tía slept in another with their baby daughter. Rosa had the third room. Her room was very small, but Rosa knew she was lucky to have her own room.

Papá and Tío also plowed farmland. They gave the owner part of the money that they earned when they sold the crop. When they had a good crop, they had enough money to buy the things the family needed. Mamá and Tía worked hard in the house. They cooked and cleaned and took care of baby Isabella. Mamá loved to work in the garden behind the house. She grew carrots and green beans and peas and potatoes and radishes and onions for the family to eat.

Rosa loved to hear the stories of when her family lived in Mexico. She did not want to give up speaking Spanish. She even wanted to visit Mexico someday. But she would never go to the best school if she did not speak English. Only white children went to the best school. In the Mexican school, children copied the alphabet and learned to read a few words in the morning. Then they played. After lunch they worked on addition and subtraction for a little while. Then they played some more.

Rosa loved to play, too, but she could play at home. At school, she wanted to learn to read. She wanted to learn about the world. She wanted to learn about history. She did not want to jump rope at school.

After school, Maria said, "Let's walk home together."

Rosa shook her head. "You go on, Maria. I don't feel like walking fast."

All the other children passed Rosa on the way home. School was two miles from her house. In the winter, if she did not walk fast, she felt as if her nose would freeze and break off. Now the winter winds had stopped blowing. Springtime was warmer. Soon it would be summer, and Rosa would feel as if she would melt into a puddle.

Rosa shuffled home, kicking her shoes in the dusty soil. Spring was warmer than winter, but the air was always full of dust. For the last two years, Texas had not had enough rain. Other states had the same problem. Without water, the ground dried up. When spring winds came, they blew the soil away. Papá was already worried that the soil was not good enough to plant a wheat crop this year.

Rosa turned down the short road to her house. She could see Mamá hanging wash in the backyard. Mamá worked hard to keep everything clean. When the dust blew in, it covered all the floors and walls and tables and chairs and beds in the house. Sometimes Rosa thought Mamá should stop trying so hard, because it was impossible to keep things clean.

"You look sad, *mi hija*," Mamá said. "What is wrong?"

"Mamá, you must do something about my school!" Rosa exclaimed. "Señora Gonzalez is teaching lessons I learned three years ago. I want to learn new things."

"Maybe she teaches these lessons because the other children do not know them." Mamá pinned one of Papá's shirts to the clothesline.

"No, Mamá, I don't think so."

"Then what do you think, mi hija?"

Rosa stood up straight and said boldly, "I think she is not a real teacher. She does not care if we learn or not."

"Rosa! Show respect for your teacher."

"I'm sorry, Mamá. But I don't want to play the whole day at school. I want to learn more than she can teach me. Will you please talk to her?"

"Rosa, I cannot do that. I am not a teacher. I do not understand education, and I am very busy."

"Please, Mamá!"

"Rosita, not everyone has to go to school. When I was your age in Mexico, I did not go to school anymore. School was for boys, not girls."

"That's not true here in America, Mamá!"

"Sometimes it is. Even your own brothers see that hard work is more important. Can I feed my children with a book?"

"I know everyone works hard, Mamá." Rosa held back her tears. How could Mamá be so mean? "And I would work hard at learning if I could only go to a good school."

Mamá stopped hanging shirts in the dusty air and put her hand on Rosa's cheek. "Rosita, I know this is something you want very much. But it is not something that I can give you."

From her basket on the wooden porch, Isabella began to cry. Mamá sighed. "The baby has not had a good nap all day. Your tía needs to rest."

Rosa turned toward the porch. "I will take care of the baby."

Rosa carried two-month-old Isabella close to her chest all afternoon to keep the baby quiet. Tía was very tired. She had not gotten strong again after the baby was born. More and more, she was tired or did not feel well. Sometimes she coughed all night. Rosa wanted Tía to sleep until supper, so she took the baby outside where Tía would not hear her cries.

When suppertime came, Papá, Tío, and the boys came in from the fields. They were tired, too.

Papá and Tío got up before the sun rose every day. After doing a few chores, they woke up Rosa's brothers.

Téodoro was seventeen. Papá treated him like a man because he could work as hard as a man. But Mamá liked to take care of him as if he were still a little boy.

Rafaél was fifteen. He was not as strong as Téodoro, but he

loved to be outside. Rafaél hated going to school. He used to spend all day looking out the windows, wishing he could be in the field. One day he told Papá he did not want to go to school anymore.

Juan was fourteen. He stopped going to school when he was twelve. He wanted to work with the men, and Papá needed some extra help. Juan liked to take care of animals. If one of the pigs or cows was sick, Papá always called Juan to help him decide what to do.

Rosa sat in a chair, holding Isabella, as her brothers washed up for supper. Mamá was wiping the dust off the dishes. Even though the women washed the dishes after each meal, the plates and cups were full of dust by the next meal. Rosa remembered the dust storms from the last two years. This year, 1934, would not be any different. Already they had seen two small dust storms, and Rosa knew many more would blow across their fields before the summer was over.

Tío went upstairs to check on Tía Natalia. Tía was too tired to come down for supper. Mamá fixed a plate to keep warm and take up to Tía later.

After supper while Mamá and Rosa cleaned up the kitchen, Papá, Tío, and the boys went out again for evening chores. Some of the cows had to be milked, and the chickens were clacking for food. When the men finished their chores, they would be ready to go to bed. Anyone who wanted to be a rancher or farmer had to be ready for long days in the fields and pastures.

Isabella finally fell asleep in Rosa's arms. The sleeping baby, with her thumb in her mouth, did not wake as Rosa laid her in her basket in a quiet corner of the big room. Rosa went outside. At least the dust was good for something. Each night Rosa went outside and pulled her favorite stick from the ground next to the porch. She used a stick in the dust to practice writing English words.

When she was smaller, she spelled easy words like *rat* and *cat* and *hat*. Then she learned to spell words like *table*, *farmer*, and *fields*. But those were too easy now. She thought of harder words in her head. Rosa said a word aloud over and over again to listen to the sounds it had. Then she tried to spell the word by writing in the dust with her stick. Rosa knew that if she could learn to read and write in English, she would be able to read many more books. If she could read, then Rosa could learn about anything she wanted.

Rosa stood and looked at the words she had spelled. Some of them were right. Others were wrong. But she had no one who could tell her the difference. Mamá and Papá and Téodoro went to school in Mexico. They did not know how to read and write the English words that they spoke. Rafaél and Juan made fun of her because she wanted to go to school. Tía was busy with the baby and often sick. Tío was busy with the farm and taking care of Tía.

No one could help her learn.

As the sun went down, Rosa got ready to go to bed. Usually Mamá helped her move Isabella's basket to Tía's room for the night. But tonight Rosa did not think that was a good idea.

"Tía is sick, Mamá. If she starts coughing, Isabella will wake up and start crying. Then Tío will have two people to take care of in the night. Let Isabella sleep in my room."

"You are a kind girl," Mamá said.

Lying in her own bed, Rosa listened to the quick breathing of the sleeping baby. Rosa was sure to be quiet, but she did not go to sleep right away. She thought about Papá's Bible on the shelf in the big room. Did Papá ever read that book? Did he believe that God could answer prayers?

"I believe," Rosa said to herself. "I believe God does not want me to work in the fields when I grow up. He wants me to be a teacher. But how can I be a teacher if I have no one to teach me?"

Sleep came at last to Rosa. The next thing she knew, it was dawn, and Isabella was squawking for someone to feed her.

CHAPTER 2

Dust Everywhere

Rosa looked at the three hooks on the wall of her room. Her five cotton dresses hung on those three hooks. She was lucky to have five dresses. Before, Rosa had only two dresses. Then Tía surprised her by cutting down some of her own dresses so Rosa would have some pretty clothes.

Rosa used to like to choose what to wear. Sometimes she borrowed a scarf from Mamá or a belt from Tía to make her dress prettier. It did not seem to matter anymore. All her clothes were covered with dust. Starting in the spring, the winds blew fiercely across the open plains of Texas where she lived. It was almost the end of April, and the winds had been blowing for weeks. But no rain came. The soil was too dry and blew away in the wind. The fields did not have enough soil, but everywhere else had too much soil.

Wind turned the dirt into fine dust so tiny that it could go through even the smallest hole. Mamá tried to keep the dust out of the house. If she saw a crack in the wall, she stuffed a rag in the crack. Old flour sacks went around the edges of the windows. Mamá saved socks with holes and towels and old clothes to stuff into every crack she could find. Rosa thought that Mamá found more cracks every day. *Soon she will want to put my dresses into the cracks,* Rosa thought.

Still the dust came. The house was full of dusty clothes, dusty dishes, dusty furniture. Sometimes Rosa thought her brothers should just shovel up the dirt in the house and take it back out to the fields. Or maybe Mamá and Tía could put all the dirt in one room and plant their garden inside the house.

Rosa chose a dusty red dress and put it on. Mamá would call her to breakfast soon.

Downstairs, Rosa slipped into her usual chair. The dishes in the sink told her that Papá and the boys had already eaten. By now they were chasing cattle and trying to find something for the cows to eat. With no soil, there was no grass. In the grazing pastures, only tumbleweeds grew.

"Where is Tía?" Rosa asked.

"Tía is a little tired, so she went back to bed."

"I heard her coughing last night," Rosa said.

Mamá did not answer. Rosa knew that meant Mamá was worried. Tía was a little better in the winter. She did not like the cold air, but she did not cough so much. Now in the spring when the winds blew, Tía covered her face with a wet handkerchief. This helped keep the dust out of her mouth and nose. Still, Rosa knew Tía was getting sicker.

"Eat your breakfast, hija," Mamá said as she set a glass of fresh milk and a bowl of beans in front of Rosa.

"Beans for breakfast again?" Rosa whined.

"Be grateful. Eat them before the dust gets them."

"Yes, Mamá."

The glass Mamá gave Rosa had a saucer on top of it. If Mamá did not cover the glass, the milk would be too dirty for Rosa to drink. Rosa carefully moved the saucer, took a gulp of milk, and put the saucer back on the glass as swiftly as she could. She was tired of eating beans, no matter how many different ways Mamá tried to fix them. She ate quickly so that she would not be eating a bowl of dirt. When she finished, Rosa put her dishes in the sink.

"After school, I will watch Isabella," Rosa offered.

"That is very kind of you, hija," Mamá said. She smiled at her only daughter. Mamá had a wet rag in one hand and was already wiping dust off the table again.

Rosa picked up her lunch bucket. She knew that Mamá had made her a bean sandwich, because that was what she ate every day. Rosa walked down the short road in front of their house and began the two-mile walk to school in town. In the first field, she saw Papá and Tío and Téodoro. They picked up dirt and let it run through their fingers.

"Good morning, Papá!" Rosa called out.

"Rosita, how are you this morning?"

"I am fine, Papá." Rosa slowed and walked along the fence to see what Papá was doing.

Papá shook his head as the soil blew through his fingers. "The dirt is too thin. It has no topsoil at all anymore."

"It will rain soon," Tío said. Tío always believed that the drought would be over soon. Already, two years had passed with very little rain. Surely the drought would not last another year.

"We will need a great deal of rain. I do not think there will be enough. We will waste our seed if we try to plant."

"But if we do not plant, then we have no hope of a crop," Tío argued. "If we have no crop, we have no money."

"But at least we will have seed to use when the rains come."

"It will be too late by then," Tío insisted. "We are good farmers. We can take care of the crop, and with a good crop we can afford a tractor. Then next year will be even better."

Papá smiled at Tío as he shook his head. "José, when I married your sister, I knew you were stubborn. But I did not think you would be this stubborn."

"We will plant," Tío said. "And we will harvest."

Papá looked up at the sky, and Rosa followed his gaze. She saw clouds, but they were not rain clouds. They were more dust clouds. Already, the morning air was hazy. The dust clouds would roll through in the afternoon, and it would be too dark to see anything, even with a light.

"Okay, José. We will wait a few more days, and we will try to plant. Téodoro, make sure the plow is working well, please."

"Yes, Papá," Téodoro said as he started across the field to the barn. Tío followed him.

Papá turned to Rosa. "Are you going to school, hija?"

"Yes, Papá."

"You love school more than anyone else I know," Papá said. "You have a good mind."

"Papá, do you think school is only for boys?"

Papá looked thoughtful. "School is not for everyone. We have plenty of work that does not need book learning. But times are changing. If you want to go to school, then you should go."

Rosa looked down and dragged one foot slowly through the dirt. "I do want to go to school, Papá. But I want to go to a good school. The Mexican school is not a good school."

"We are Mexicans, Rosita. You can learn from the other children in the Mexican school."

"No, Papá, I can't. They don't want to learn. They only want to play."

"It is not so bad to play sometimes."

"School is for learning, Papá. I want to learn. I want to go to the white school."

Papá looked at her sharply. "Rosa! You do not know what you are asking."

"It's not fair, Papá. At the white school, they have books and paper and four teachers. They even study at home at night."

"When do they have time to help with the work at home?" Papá asked.

Rosa shrugged. "I don't know. But if they can do it, I can do it. Please talk to the teachers at the white school and ask them to let me go there."

Papá shook his head firmly. "No, Rosita, I cannot do that. I cannot put the family in danger just because you want to go to school."

"You mean it would make the white people angry if I asked to go to their school, because they think Mexicans are stupid? I am not stupid, Papá. I can learn if someone will teach me."

Papá put his hand on Rosa's head. "Of course you are not stupid. But to go to the white school—you ask for something very big."

"Then please talk to la maestra. Maybe she can give me some extra lessons. I will stay inside and do them while the other children play."

"That is the job of Señora Gonzalez. She knows what you need to learn much better than I do. You already read better than I do. What more can I ask of her?"

"Please, Papá."

"You will be late for school, Rosa. I will see you this afternoon." Papá turned and began to walk across the field. He had that look on his face that meant his mind was made up.

Rosa walked to town. As she got close to the school, she saw the other children playing already. She knew Señora Gonzalez would let them play for a long time before she called them in for lessons.

"Why should I go to school there?" she asked aloud. "I will go to the white school."

Instead of turning toward the Mexican school, Rosa turned and walked in another direction. She knew where the white school was, and that's where she was going. Swinging her lunch bucket as she walked confidently, Rosa went where she had always wanted to go.

CHAPTER 3

New Friends, New Hopes

All day, Rosa stayed outside Lowell School, where the white children attended. A gray metal fence kept her off the play yard, but she could see through the fence. When the children came outside for recess or lunch, she moved to a corner. She wanted to watch, but she did not want anyone to see her. While they played, the children chattered in English. Rosa listened for any new words and imagined how to spell them.

When the children went back inside, Rosa looked through an open window. The children had desks and books and pencils. No one played inside the school the way they did at the Mexican school. If she listened carefully, maybe she would be able to hear the teacher talking. Maybe she would hear about a country far away. Maybe she would learn some new math. Most of the time, she could not hear anything, but she kept trying. Rosa imagined what it would be like to go to this school.

Rosa went back to the school behind the fence two more times. Nothing would make her happier than to be able to go inside one day. If she could look at the books and papers, she was sure she would learn and learn.

At the end of the third day, Rosa slowly walked home. At home, Mamá and Papá wanted her to help more. She helped Papá plant an acre of potatoes. The air was so full of dirt that they could hardly see each other as they dug holes. Rosa wore a scarf over her nose and mouth the whole time. Mamá needed help on washday because Tía was too weak. Rosa helped scrub the clothes over the washboard to loosen the dirt. Then she dipped them in a kettle of boiling water. Mamá hung them on the line to dry. It seemed to Rosa that the clothes just got dirty all over again before they even got dry. Every day, the air was thick with dust.

Now the baby was getting sick, too. A cough shook her tiny chest and made her cry. Rosa tried to take care of Isabella. She cleaned the dust out of one room at a time and put the baby in the clean room. She hung a light blanket over Isabella's basket to keep the dirt out. The little one struggled to breathe, but she seemed better under the blanket. When Tío looked at his baby daughter, Rosa saw his sadness, and she felt even sadder herself.

While she helped Mamá and Papá, Rosa thought about the school for white children. Mamá and Papá did not know she had stopped going to the school for Mexican children. If Papá found out she did not go to school at all, he would say she should just stay home. There was a lot of work to do. Mamá and Tía needed her help. So Rosa was not sure she could go back to the school behind the fence many more times. What if Señora Gonzalez asked Mamá why Rosa was not in school? She did not even want to imagine what Mamá would say. Papá would be so disappointed Rosa would hardly be able to stand it. She decided she would go just one more time, and then she would return to the Mexican school.

Rosa arrived early the next morning to watch the white children come to the schoolyard and meet their friends. She listened as they played and called to one another. When the bell rang, they got in lines behind their teachers. Four teachers in one school! The younger students had their own classrooms instead of being together with the older students the way they were at Rosa's school. After the children went inside, Rosa settled in to watch and listen for the morning. She had a favorite place to sit where the dust was not too bad.

"What are you doing out here, child?"

Rosa spun around and blushed. She jumped to her feet and furiously beat the dust out of her dress.

"Never mind your dress. Why are you out here? You should be in school."

The young woman speaking to Rosa was well-dressed with nice shoes and a hat. Rosa did not think the woman was rich, but she took very good care of her clothes. Her golden hair was twisted at the sides of her head and pinned under her hat, and her face gleamed through the dust in the air. She did not look like a teacher in the usual plain dress and sensible shoes. No one had ever looked so beautiful to Rosa.

"I'm sorry, ma'am. I will go now." Rosa turned to walk toward the Mexican school. She hoped her English sounded right.

"Where are you going, young lady?"

"To my school."

"Isn't this your school?"

"No, ma'am." Couldn't the lady see that Rosa was Mexican? Everyone knew that Mexican children did not go to school with white children.

"Why aren't you at your school already?" the lady asked. "Aren't they having class today?"

Rosa looked down at the ground. She was not sure what to say. Papá did not like it when she talked to strangers, especially white strangers.

"Don't be shy," the lady said. Her voice was softer now. "Tell me why you are here."

Rosa could not hold in her words any longer. "I am here because I want to learn! At my school, we play too much. No one cares if we learn! I want a school with a real teacher, and books, and maps."

"I have heard that the Mexican children play more than they study." The lady looked thoughtful for a moment. Then she put out her hand to shake Rosa's. "My name is Mrs. Madden. I used to be a teacher."

Rosa shook Mrs. Madden's hand shyly. "I'm sorry. I should not have spoken like that."

"There is nothing wrong with the way you spoke. Clearly, you have strong opinions. Now, tell me your name."

"My name is Rosa, ma'am."

"Don't you have a last name?"

"Sanchez. My name is Rosa Margarita Sanchez."

"Well, Rosa Margarita Sanchez, I am very glad to meet you. I would like to talk more about your school." She pointed down the road. "My husband is the minister at that church right over there, and we live next door. Would you like to come to my house for milk and cookies?"

Cookies! Mamá never had extra flour for cookies. But Rosa shook her head. "I do not think Mamá and Papá would like that."

Mrs. Madden swatted herself in the forehead. "Of course not.

I am a stranger. But I don't have to remain a stranger. Why don't you introduce me to your parents?"

"You want to meet Mamá and Papá?"

"I certainly do."

"I am very sorry. I did not mean to cause trouble. I will go to my own school right away." Rosa turned to leave again and began to run.

"Rosa!" Mrs. Madden called. "Rosa, please come back. You don't understand."

Rosa stopped running and turned around, but she did not go close to Mrs. Madden.

"I do not want to get you in trouble, Rosa," Mrs. Madden said. "I want to help you."

"Help me?"

"Yes. You want to learn. And I used to be a teacher. Perhaps we can help each other."

"Papá will say no." Papá never spoke to white people except about ranch business. He did not like to try to speak English.

"We will ask and see what he says."

"But we have no money. There are no crops, and there aren't many animals left."

"I understand," Mrs. Madden said. "The drought has hurt everyone. I am not asking you to pay me. But if you'd like, you could help me take care of my little boy."

Rosa's eyes lit up. "You have a little boy?"

"Yes. His name is Henry."

"I help take care of my little cousin. Her name is Isabella."

"Then I am sure you will be a wonderful help to me. Now, tell me how to find your house, and I will come after school."

"I'm not sure. I don't think Papá will like this."

"I will talk to your papá. I will explain that this is my idea."

"Papá does not know I have not been going to my own school," Rosa said quietly.

Mrs. Madden nodded. "I understand your problem. I will take care of that, as well."

"But you do not know my papá," Rosa answered.

"I assure you I can be extraordinarily persuasive."

Rosa looked down at her dusty shoes. "I am sorry. I do not know these words."

Mrs. Madden smiled. "It means I will explain to your father, and he will understand and give his permission. Just tell me where you live."

Rosa was so nervous she was shaking. She explained to Mrs. Madden how to find her family's home. When Mrs. Madden left, Rosa scampered off to her own school for the rest of the day. After school, she rushed home instead of walking slowly. She wanted to be there before Mrs. Madden arrived.

Rosa was afraid Papá would be far away in one of the fields. But he was in the barn. She peeked in a window to make sure he stayed there.

Mrs. Madden arrived in a car. On the seat beside her was a little boy with shiny white hair. *That's Henry,* Rosa thought. Henry was older than Isabella. He was old enough to pull himself up in the seat and lean against his mother. Soon he would learn to walk. Rosa thought she would like taking care of Henry.

Rosa watched from behind the barn as Mrs. Madden lifted Henry out of the car and walked to the front door. She knocked, and Mamá opened the door. Mamá and Mrs. Madden talked for a few minutes. Rosa was not sure Mamá understood everything Mrs. Madden said. Mamá led Mrs. Madden inside the house, then came back out and went to the barn. Papá followed Mamá back to the house with a puzzled look on his face.

Rosa's stomach lurched and tumbled. She had never been this nervous in her whole life. A few minutes felt like days as she waited.

Finally, Mrs. Madden came out, smiling. Papá was looking around for Rosa, so Rosa stepped out from behind the barn. Mrs. Madden walked straight toward her.

"Your papá has agreed, Rosa."

"He has?"

"Yes, and your mamá as well. You may come to my house every day after school. First we will have a lesson, and then you will take care of Henry while I prepare supper for my husband."

"Yes, ma'am!" Rosa grinned at Mamá and Papá.

"Here is my address." Mrs. Madden handed Rosa a small piece of paper. "I will expect you tomorrow right after school. Be prompt!"

"Yes, ma'am!"

Rosa thought she must be dreaming. Could this really be happening? She was going to get private lessons from a real teacher!

The next day, Rosa watched the clock carefully. A few times, she thought the hands of the clock might be stopped. She stared and stared until they moved. Rosa stayed inside, watching the clock while the other children played outside in the afternoon. In only one more hour, she would begin learning, really learning!

Suddenly all the children rushed back inside, coughing and covering their faces. Oh no! A dust storm! Rosa looked out the window at the billowing dark clouds. This was going to be a big one, she could tell. Already she could barely see anything out of the window. The school building had many cracks and holes. Nothing would keep the dust out.

La maestra dampened some clean rags in a bucket of water and began to hand them out to the children. Rosa put the damp rag over her face like all the other children did. As the storm blew closer, Rosa's heart sank. She held the rag over her face with one hand and put the other hand in the pocket of her dress. The little piece of paper with Mrs. Madden's address was there. Rosa had touched it so many times during the day that it was getting worn out. She did not even need the paper because she had memorized the address.

But she would never be able to go to Mrs. Madden's house today. Señora Gonzalez would not let her leave in the middle of the dust storm. Everyone knew that in a dust storm, the air was so dark you could not see where you were going. Even if you had a light, it did not matter very much. The air was too dark to see through and too dusty to breathe. Dust storms could last for hours—or even days. One time, the children stayed at school all night, waiting for the storm to pass.

Rosa pulled the rag up over her eyes so no one would see the tears sliding down her cheeks.

CHAPTER 4

Hurry Home

Rosa moved the wet cloth off her face to look at the clock. If the dust storm had not come, she would be at Mrs. Madden's house right now. She would be finished with her first lesson, and she would be playing with little Henry while his mother cooked supper.

Rosa wondered what her first lesson would be. Perhaps Mrs. Madden had some books for her to read or an atlas to look at. Rosa also wondered what Mrs. Madden's home would be like. Would she have pretty curtains and tablecloths? Would her plates and cups have flowers on them? Did she sew the quilts for the beds herself?

But Rosa was stuck at the school. It was no use asking Señora Gonzalez if she could leave. The storm was not so bad, but it was still too dangerous to go outside.

Rosa could not help worrying about Mamá and Tía and baby Isabella. Were they inside the house with wet rags over their faces? Had Mamá used the extra sheets to cover the furniture? This storm would make Tía cough all night. Isabella would cry because she did not want to stay in her basket under the blanket. She wanted someone to hold her. Papá and the boys might be out in the pastures, crouching to the ground and trying to keep the wind out of their faces.

The clock ticked slowly. Every few minutes Rosa peeked at it, hoping the hands would move faster. All the children in the school wanted to go home. When they could not play, school was not a fun place to be. Some of the younger children were frightened and whimpered while the storm raged. Finally the sky began to get lighter. Miguel asked la maestra if they could go home. Then Roderigo asked, then Maria, then Juanita. Each time Señora Gonzalez shook her head. No. It was not safe yet. Rosa watched the clock. Finally, when Mierta asked to go home, la maestra nodded.

After four hours, the wind had calmed down. The air was heavy with dust, but if the children were careful, they could walk home safely. If they did not go soon, nightfall would come. Rosa did not want to spend the whole night in the school.

Rosa dashed out the door as soon as Señora Gonzalez gave permission. She held the hem of her long skirt up to her face as she ran. Running in the dirt reminded Rosa of running in snow. The storm had piled up the dirt in the road so high that it was up to her knees. The little children could hardly walk at all. Older brothers and sisters picked them up to carry them. Once Rosa stumbled and fell face-first into the dirt. Spitting out dirt, she scrambled to her feet and kept going.

She could hardly see the road ahead of her. Instead, she watched the trees along the side of the road. Not many trees grew there, but Rosa knew the ones that did. She knew which tree meant that she should turn left and which tree meant that she should keep going straight. One by one, the children turned off to their homes. Rosa had forgotten all about Mrs. Madden and Henry. She only wanted to be home!

Mamá and Papá would be worried about her. Every time a storm came while Rosa was at school, they waited and watched for her to make it home safely. Each time, they prayed that no one in the family would get hurt.

Rosa started to cough. With every breath, she pulled dust into her throat and lungs. Fine grains of sand in the air stung her cheeks. She pressed the hem of her skirt closer to her face. Her eyes squinted through the dusty air to see where she was going.

At last she saw her house. The wash on the line was black with dirt. Mamá would have to wash everything again. Rosa raced as fast as she could to the house and pulled open the big front door.

"Mamá!" Rosa called. "Mamá! Tía! Are you here?" She raced from room to room, looking for Mamá and Tía and Isabella. They were not in the kitchen or the big room or the back porch. Rosa climbed the stairs. "Mamá! Tía!"

She found them in a bedroom, huddled under a blanket. The blanket was dark with heavy dust, but under it, Mamá's and Tía's faces were almost clean.

"Rosa!" Mamá threw off the blanket and opened her arms to hug her daughter. "Rosa, are you all right?"

Rosa wrapped her arms around Mamá's neck. "I'm fine, Mamá. How is everybody here?" Rosa lifted the blanket on baby Isabella's basket to see her little cousin sound asleep.

"Your papá and tío are in the barn with the milking cows. You know how much dirt comes in through the walls of the barn. It will be a lot of work to shovel it all out. Your brothers are looking for the animals. They don't want the chickens to die from the dust. We need the eggs those chickens give us. Juan is worried about one of the pigs who is not moving around much these days."

"Yes, Mamá. I will help clean up. Shall I begin with the kitchen?"

Mamá sighed. "Yes, we will begin with the kitchen. We will have to sweep and wash all the dishes before we can eat supper."

"I will help, too," Tía said. She pushed the blanket off her knees and reached for Isabella's basket.

Tía coughed, and her shoulders shuddered.

"Tía!" Rosa exclaimed. "That sounds like it hurts!"

"Yes, it hurts. But it hurts me more to know that I am too sick to help."

"We want you to get well, Tía."

"I know. You are both very sweet. But I want to help clean up." Tía coughed so hard that she could hardly breathe.

"You need a damp cloth," Rosa declared. "I'll get you one."

"Thank you. Then I will come downstairs. If I don't have the strength to sweep, at least I can help cook."

Rosa went downstairs and opened a drawer in the kitchen. Even the towels and cloths in the drawer were brown with dust. She rinsed a cloth in clean water, wrung it out, and took it to Tía.

Mamá came back downstairs with Rosa this time. She carried Isabella's basket. Tía wanted to come down, but Mamá would not let her.

Rosa's brothers burst through the back door. Mamá raised her eyebrows to ask if the animals were all right.

"We found all the chickens in the pen, Mamá," Juan said. "They are clacking up a storm of their own, but they are fine."

"God has blessed us," Mamá said. "And the pigs?"

Téodoro nodded. "Yes, the pigs are fine, as well. We had to uncover Old Hombre. He did not have sense to get out of the way of the storm, and the dust almost buried him."

"He is old and tired," Mamá said. "It is difficult for him to move quickly."

"What about the range cattle?" Rosa asked.

Rafaél shook his head. "Most of them are out in the pastures. Soon it will be too dark to look for them. We will have to hope they survive until tomorrow."

Everyone was silent. They all knew that every time one of the range cattle died, the family lost many dollars. They had one less cow to sell to the meatpacking plants in Dalhart or to sell to ranchers in other states. The owner of the ranch would take the value of the cow out of their earnings. Sometimes a storm came so fast and hard that it buried cattle before anyone could bring them to safety. Workers looked for days to find all the cattle roaming the ranch.

Rosa went to the corner of the kitchen to get the broom. Slowly she began to push the dirt into piles near the back door. She had done this many times before. Often she wished that she had a shovel instead of a broom. The dirt that came through the walls of the house was thick and deep. Moving it with just a broom was hard work. Even if she had six pairs of arms and twelve brooms, cleaning up would take a long time.

Mamá found a cardboard box and tore off the flaps. She used them to scoop up dirt from the table and counters and the stove and carried the dirt to the back door.

"If only we could plant something in all this dirt," Mamá said. "It is such a waste to have so much dirt in the house and no good soil in the fields."

They worked together silently for a long time. While she rested from pushing the broom, Rosa could hear Tía coughing upstairs.

Isabella stirred in her basket, and Rosa peeked in and smiled at her. Isabella smiled back and began to wave her hands at Rosa's face.

"Isabella doesn't know we had a dust storm," Rosa said.

"She is too little to understand," Mamá said. "She just wants someone to keep her safe. She is lucky to have you."

Rosa smiled at Mamá's compliment. Inside, she thought, *Sometimes I wish I were too little to understand. Then I could just learn and grow like you, little Isabella.*

"Rosa, mi hija," Mamá said, "it's getting late. I must make supper. The men will be hungry."

"You cook, Mamá. Make the biggest supper you can. I will finish cleaning."

"It's too late to start cooking, and everyone is tired. We'll just have cold sandwiches."

That meant lard sandwiches, Rosa knew. Eating pork fat smeared on a piece of bread was better than being hungry, but she sure didn't like lard sandwiches.

They worked silently for a while. Finally Mamá spoke.

"I am sorry that you did not get to have your lesson today, mi hija."

"Thank you, Mamá. I really wanted to go to Mrs. Madden's house. But I can go tomorrow. I have waited a long time to learn. I can be patient one more day." *Please, no more dust storms!* Rosa thought.

Just then, Papá and Tío came in.

"I am so glad that everyone is safe," Papá said. He laid his hand on Rosa's head affectionately.

"How is Natalia?" Tío asked.

"She's upstairs," Mamá answered. "She wanted to help clean up, but I would not allow it."

"Thank you, *hermana*," Tío said. "You are taking very good care of my wife."

"We are all taking care of each other," Mamá said.

Tío sighed and peeked into Isabella's basket. "Soon things will get better," Tío said. "We have seen many storms worse than this one. This may be the last one. The spring rains will come, and we will plant a good crop. In the fall we will have a good harvest."

Tío turned and went upstairs to see Tía.

Rosa watched Mamá and Papá look at each other. Tío often said that things would get better soon. Papá was not so sure.

CHAPTER 5

The Essay

Rosa ran to Mrs. Madden's house on the last day of school. Each day, she could hardly wait to get there. Mrs. Madden kept a special pile of books for Rosa, and Rosa could choose what she wanted to read. If the words were too hard, Mrs. Madden helped her sound them out. Then they talked about the people and ideas in the books. Some of the books were true stories, and some of them were made-up stories. Rosa liked the made-up stories best.

Rosa learned about adding, subtracting, multiplying, and dividing. Mrs. Madden made learning math fun. Sometimes, she wrote numbers on a piece of paper for Rosa to work on. But sometimes, she made up little stories with numbers in them, and Rosa had to concentrate hard as she listened. Then it was her turn to write down the numbers from the story and decide if she should add or subtract, multiply or divide. How much money did Mr. Peters make when he sold his cattle? How many baskets of fruit will the church need for the picnic? How long will it take to drive from Texas to California?

The spelling words were Rosa's favorite part of her lessons. She learned many new English words, and Mrs. Madden made up the silliest sentences. Then Mrs. Madden asked Rosa to teach her how to say the words in Spanish. At home, Rosa began to say English words to baby Isabella. She hoped Isabella would learn to speak English perfectly.

School was out for the summer. Now Rosa could go to Mrs. Madden's house and study while Henry took a nap. Papá said she still had to do her chores in the morning and the evening. Mamá did not want her to bother Mrs. Madden too much. Rosa did not think she was a bother to Mrs. Madden.

Rosa was breathless by the time she got to the Madden home and knocked on the front door. Mrs. Madden opened the door and smiled.

"Rosa! I'm so glad you could come."

"School is out now!" Rosa exclaimed.

"I know! Now you can work twice as hard at your lessons."

"And I can learn twice as much."

"I hope so. What shall we start with today?"

Rosa chose a book about the history of the United States. She had never been anywhere outside of northwest Texas, the part of Texas that looked like the handle of a cooking pan, but she knew that the United States was an enormous country. Rosa wondered who the first settlers were, and she wanted to read about the Revolutionary War and the Declaration of Independence. Stories about pioneers in the Old West were so exciting that Rosa could imagine herself being there. For hundreds of years, families came to the New World with hope for a better life, just the way the Sanchez family came from Mexico.

Mrs. Madden asked Rosa to read aloud so she could help her pronounce the words correctly. Henry sat quietly in his mother's lap as if he were learning to read, too. At school, the clock seemed to stand still. At Mrs. Madden's house, the time went by so fast that it was time for supper before Rosa realized it.

"You seem very interested in American history," Mrs. Madden said.

"I love to learn about this country," Rosa responded. "It's not the same as the stories my brothers tell me about Mexico. When I read a book like this, I learn a lot of things I never knew before."

"Would you like to take the book home with you?" Mrs. Madden asked.

Rosa's eyes widened. "You would let me take your book home?" She could hardly believe her ears. She had never had an English book at home before.

"Of course," Mrs. Madden answered, laughing. "Read some more chapters, and we'll talk about them tomorrow."

"Thank you, Mrs. Madden. No one has ever been this kind to me before. Thank you very much."

"It's my pleasure, Rosa," Mrs. Madden said. "It's fun to have such an enthusiastic student."

Holding the book carefully, Rosa went home to her chores. She had to feed the chickens and sweep the kitchen. First she went upstairs to see if Tía needed anything, and then she peeked into Isabella's basket. They were both sleeping, so Rosa crept to her own room and made sure Mrs. Madden's book was safe under her pillow. Then she went back downstairs, trying not to make the steps creak.

She swept the kitchen floor, then went to the barn to find something to feed the chickens. Tío tried to keep bags of grain to feed the chickens. Sometimes he had oats or corn or wheat. But the drought had made it so hard to grow crops that even the chickens did not have enough to eat. Mamá sometimes gave them dried bread or leftover rice and beans. Mamá never threw away a crumb of food. Instead, she tossed it into the bucket in the barn to feed the chickens or the pigs.

Rosa did her best to spread the chicken feed around the pen so that the bigger chickens did not eat everything before the smaller ones came to eat. Then she stepped out of the pen and watched the chickens picking at the ground and grabbing bits of food with their beaks.

Mamá would call everyone for supper soon. Rosa lifted her eyes to the sky. It had been so long since she had seen a truly clear sky. With the drought and dust storms, the sky was always brownish and heavy-looking.

Rosa heard a scratching noise and turned her head to look behind her. When she heard the sound again, she knew it came from a nearby tree. Rosa scanned the branches until she saw the bird. It chirped while it tidied the walls of a nest. Birds made nests out of tiny sticks and long grass. But not this bird. So little grass grew in the pastures. Even the trees were too dry to grow new branches. The bird had made its nest out of pieces of barbed-wire fences. Rosa did not think that a barbed-wire nest would be very comfortable for the baby birds when they hatched. But what could she do? She felt more sad for the bird with the metal nest than she did for herself.

Rosa soon fell into a pattern for the summer. After cleaning up the breakfast dishes each morning, she went to Mrs. Madden's house. While Henry took his morning nap, Rosa studied. She was full of questions! But Mrs. Madden never seemed to get tired of answering them. When Henry woke up, Rosa played with him for a while so Mrs. Madden could wipe the dust off the tables or prepare lunch for her husband.

"Henry has a question," Rosa said one day as she held Henry on her hip.

Mrs. Madden smiled. "Is that so?" She was wiping dust off dishes in the kitchen.

"Yes, ma'am. Henry wants to know why the American flag has thirteen stripes and forty-eight stars."

"Well, let's see. You can tell Henry that the stripes are for the thirteen original colonies, and the forty-eight stars represent the forty-eight states in the Union."

"I think Henry understands now," Rosa answered.

They played this game day after day. Rosa said Henry had a question, and Mrs. Madden answered it. Then Rosa repeated the answer to Henry with an exaggerated voice that made him giggle.

One day, Mrs. Madden handed Rosa a piece of paper. "Can you read this by yourself?"

Rosa studied the words on the page. " 'We are pleased to. . . a—announce the theme for this year's. . .con—test. Essays must. . . answer the question, "Why do I love America?" ' "

"Very good," Mrs. Madden said. "Every year the town has this contest. The children write short essays to answer a question, and the winner gets a prize."

"I've never heard of it," Rosa said, puzzled.

"Rosa," Mrs. Madden said with a serious tone, "how brave can you be?"

"Why? Is the contest dangerous?"

"It might be dangerous for you. No Mexican children have ever entered the contest before."

"Oh." Rosa was disappointed. She wanted to write an essay.

"I think you should enter, Rosa."

"But you said Mexican children are not allowed."

"No, I said no Mexican children have ever entered. I see nothing in the rules that limits the background of the children who participate."

"Do you really think I should enter?"

"Yes, I do, Rosa. I believe you would write a wonderful essay."

"I do love America," Rosa said thoughtfully.

"You certainly do."

"And I would like to write an essay."

"The rules say you have to do it all on your own without any help."

"Do you really think I can?" Rosa asked. Writing an essay in English without Mrs. Madden's help would be scary.

"I believe in you with all my heart," Mrs. Madden answered.

"Then I should do it!"

Mrs. Madden clapped her hands. Then Henry clapped his. Rosa laughed.

A few days later, while Rosa worked on arithmetic, someone knocked on Mrs. Madden's front door. When Mrs. Madden opened the door, Rosa heard voices. She thought there were at least two men and wondered if Mrs. Madden was all right. Rosa watched as Mrs. Madden stepped out onto her front porch and closed the door behind her. Rosa supposed that was because Henry was sound asleep. Still curious, Rosa moved to the open window. She recognized Mr. Decker from the granary in town and Mr. Elliot from the cattle auction.

"I won't have you speaking about that delightful child that way," Mrs. Madden said sternly. "You don't even know her. She's lovely."

"She's Mexican," Mr. Decker said.

"So what?" Mrs. Madden challenged him.

With a gasp, Rosa realized they were arguing about her. The last thing she wanted was to get Mrs. Madden into trouble.

"So why did she sign up to enter the contest?" Mr. Elliot asked.

"Why shouldn't she?" Mrs. Madden was not giving up. "I find nothing in the rules that forbids her from entering."

"Miz Madden, with all due respect, we've got our ways. I understand you're the preacher's wife, but you ain't been in this town very long."

"I've been here long enough to know you're being unfair to the Mexican children!" Mrs. Madden exclaimed.

"Well, ma'am, I beg to differ," Mr. Decker said. "We've made sure they have a school of their own, after all."

"A school where they don't learn but play all day."

"That ain't true, Miz Madden," objected Mr. Elliot, as he twisted his mustache between two fingers.

"It most certainly is. You have deprived a little girl with a wonderful mind by not giving her a teacher to challenge her."

"I hear she's been studying with you."

"That's right. She's got one of the most curious minds I've ever seen in my years of teaching. You may as well know that I intend to make sure that when school opens again in the fall, all the children will go to school together."

"What exactly do you mean by that, Miz Madden?" Mr. Decker spoke with a harsh tone.

44

"You know what I mean," Mrs. Madden answered firmly. "No more separate schools. Give them all the opportunity to learn on an equal basis. I have already spoken to the mayor and to several members of the school board."

"I can't believe they're too happy about that notion."

"Education is not supposed to make the school board happy. It's supposed to help children learn."

"We'd all be happy if things was that simple," Mr. Decker said. "But they ain't."

"They can be," Mrs. Madden insisted. "And if I have anything to say about it, they will be. Now I think it would be best if you gentlemen were on your way."

Rosa scampered back to the table where she had left her arithmetic paper.

When she came back inside, Mrs. Madden forced a smile. "I'll just get us some cold lemonade," she said.

Henry whimpered, and Rosa picked him up and held him tightly. She thought, *Henry, I sure hope your mama knows what she's doing.*

CHAPTER 6

Happy Birthday, Rosa

At first Rosa thought she should stop going to see Mrs. Madden. She did not want Mrs. Madden or Henry to be hurt. While she dreamed of going to school with the white children, she hated the thought of people being angry with the Maddens. Rosa thought Mrs. Madden was the kindest person in the world.

But Mrs. Madden insisted that Rosa keep coming every morning. All summer they kept up their lessons. Rosa learned faster and faster. The books she took home to read at night were harder and longer than the ones she started with. She began to make up math stories for Mrs. Madden to solve. Henry adored Rosa and greeted her with a slobbery kiss every day. In their own little world, the three of them looked forward to being together every day. Nothing made Rosa happier.

Still, Rosa worried. Maybe Mrs. Madden should stop talking to the mayor and the school board. Rosa was sure she was learning as much from Mrs. Madden as she would at the school with the white children. Maybe she was learning more. After all, she had her own private teacher.

When the deadline came to turn in her essay, Rosa almost told Mrs. Madden that she had lost it. But she knew Mrs. Madden would not believe that. "How brave can you be?" Mrs. Madden asked her again and again. So Rosa turned in the essay right before her birthday in the middle of the summer and waited anxiously for the judges to make their decision.

Mamá and Papá did their best to plan a party for Rosa's birthday, but no one felt like celebrating. Inside or outside, the heat was suffocating. If they were lucky enough to have ice to put in their glasses of water, it melted almost immediately. Rosa had begun to count the really hot days that were over a hundred degrees, but she lost count because there were so many. Even when she sat in the shade, she felt as if she were on fire under her skin.

Isabella was big enough now to roll over and sit up. Rosa knew babies were supposed to be curious about the world around them. But Isabella was too hot to move around very much. On the hottest days, Isabella smiled only when Rosa wiped a wet cloth over her soft skin. One day, Rosa said to Isabella, "At least you're a baby and you only have to wear a diaper." Rosa's sweat was like glue, making her own clothes stick to her skin.

Tía and Mamá cried about the vegetable garden. Rosa saw them, but they did not see her. In the past, they had grown enough vegetables to feed the whole family all summer and still have plenty for the winter. Now the well had begun to go dry, so they did not dare carry water to the garden anymore. Every drop of water was precious to the family. The carrots weren't growing into the ground the way they should. Instead, they were stubby knobs of orange just below the surface. The whole garden looked as if it had been scorched with a hot flame. Even if the skies broke out with rain for the rest of the summer, it was too late to save the garden. One day, Mamá gave up on the carrots and collected all the green carrot tops to eat with supper.

Papá stopped using his truck. Gasoline cost too much money,

and he was afraid the dust would ruin the engine. Already, the engine made strange sounds when he tried to start the truck. Papá and Tío rode horses through the fields and pastures, looking for anything the cattle could eat. Even the weeds were not growing well. Tío kept saying it would rain soon, but Papá had decided not to plant a crop. He did not want to waste the seed. They would save it for a better season or feed it to the chickens and pigs.

One night when she could not sleep because it was too hot, Rosa heard Papá tell Mamá that he was afraid he could not keep the range cattle alive much longer. Some would die from starvation before long because they had no grass to eat. Others ate the dirt and got sick from that. He was thinking of telling the owner of the ranch to sell most of the cattle now while he still could. The cattle were too thin to be worth as much as they should be, but at least they were still alive.

Papá also thought they should try to sell Old Hombre, Juan's favorite pig. The animal was still nice and fat. He could bring a good price. Or they could slaughter the pig so they could eat the meat themselves. Rosa was tired of beans and of lard sandwiches, but she hated the thought of eating Old Hombre!

The dusty winds continued to blow. Rosa could not count the times that she had washed dishes only to wash them again right before her family used them. That was the only way to be sure they could eat off of clean plates. She was constantly brushing dirt off her skirts and blouses.

Mamá made a cake for Rosa's birthday and served it outside in the late evening, after dark. Even then, it was so hot Rosa hardly wanted to move. She lay on a blanket on the ground, wishing she could feel soft green grass under her bare feet instead of stubby dust and pebbles. Isabella was beside her and had finally fallen asleep. The grown-ups sat in chairs and talked.

"The problem is the soil," Papá said. "We did not take care of it the years we had rain. We thought we would always have rain."

"That was our chance to earn some money," Tío said. "The crops were growing so well."

"We should not have tried to grow so much," Papá said. "We took all the nutrients out of the soil. Then the winds blew away the empty soil."

Téodoro spoke up. "Farming and ranching are not the only way to make a living."

"What do you mean, Téodoro?" Papá asked. "Before the rains stopped, this land was perfect for ranching and farming."

"I'm talking about California," Téodoro said. "There are jobs out there. They have plenty of rain. The trees will be heavy with fruit in the fall and winter. The farmers need people to pick the fruit and get it shipped out."

Tío nodded. "I know what you're talking about. I see the cars on the highway all the time. People pack up everything they own and go to California, looking for work."

"There are jobs there," Téodoro said again.

"But the pay is very little," Papá said. "We would all have to work, even Rosa. We would not be able to find that many jobs."

"I could find one job," Téodoro said. "I won't need much if I am by myself. I can send money back to you."

"No!" Mamá exclaimed. "No one leaves this family. Pedro, tell your son to forget about such nonsense."

Papá nodded. "I think your mamá is right, Téodoro. It is best if we stay together."

Rosa heard Téodoro's feet scuffing around in the dirt. Her brother kept silent, but she knew he would not stop thinking about California.

"The answer may come soon," Papá said. "The government is talking about holding a demonstration project right in our town."

Tío looked up, puzzled. "Demonstration? What do you mean?"

"They are learning new ways to take care of the soil and still grow crops. A demonstration project will show us all how it's done so that we can do the same thing on our own land."

"Even the government needs rain," Tío said. "We have lost our crop again this year. If we get some rain in the fall, perhaps we can grow winter wheat. We need rain, not a government project."

"Still, I would like to see it. We might learn something useful."

Rosa smiled in the dark. She was glad to hear her father say that he wanted to learn about something new. He had never said that before. Maybe now, he would understand why she wanted to go to a good school so badly.

Two days after she turned eleven years old, Rosa sat in the kitchen eating beans and rice for lunch. She was hoping Mamá would make some bread, but she knew it was too hot to have the oven on. Rosa lifted the saucer off her glass, gulped some of the liquid, and covered the glass again.

Mamá wiped dust off the table—again. That was the third time that day.

"Rosita, please go get the mail."

Rosa sighed but said, "Yes, Mamá." The mailbox was a quarter of a mile away. She had already walked to Mrs. Madden's house and back. Now it was the hottest part of the day, and she wanted to find the coolest place she could and stay there. But she finished her lunch and began the walk to the mailbox.

As soon as she opened the box and looked in, Rosa began to tremble. The box held only one envelope, and it had her name on it! Nervously, she pulled the envelope out of the box and stared at the address on the front. Yes, it was her name and address. The envelope was from the essay judges. Rosa swallowed hard as she considered whether to open the envelope or not. "It's a letter telling me I did not win," Rosa said aloud as she started to walk back toward the house. "I'll take it to Mrs. Madden tomorrow."

Halfway to the house, Rosa's curiosity got the best of her, and she gently tore off one end of the envelope. The letter slid out. She unfolded it and read it, her hands shaking the whole time.

Dear Miss Sanchez,

This letter is to inform you that you have been selected as winner of first prize in this year's civic history contest. Your thoughtful, insightful essay showed a great deal of sincerity and affection for this country. Congratulations! We will hold a ceremony to honor the first-, second-, and third-place winners. At this time, we will ask you to read your essay to the audience. We look forward to seeing you on that occasion.

Sincerely,
Civic Contest Awards Committee

Rosa picked up the hem of her skirt and ran as fast as she could in her bare feet. Now she hardly felt the heat.

"I won!" she screamed as she got close to the house. "I won!"

Mamá and Tía came outside.

"Hija, what in the world are you talking about?"

"The contest! I won the contest, Mamá! I got a letter." Rosa showed her mother the letter, even though Mamá did not know how to read English.

Mamá threw her arms around Rosa, and they spun around together. "My Rosita has won a prize!"

"I have to go show Mrs. Madden," Rosa said, breaking free of her mother's embrace. She raced down the road, not caring how much she sweated.

Mrs. Madden beamed with pride when she saw the letter.

"I knew you could do it, Rosa. You know more about American history than all the other children who entered. Of course you can explain why you love America."

"Will you go with me to the ceremony?" Rosa asked. "I won't know what to do."

"Of course, I'll go. And Henry will go, too. After all, he's the one who had all the questions about American history."

Rosa laughed. "When he's old enough to write, he will win all the contests."

"I'm so proud of you, Rosa. Now the school board will have to listen to me. They will see what happens when any student works as hard as you have. May I have this letter to show to the mayor?"

Rosa was so flushed she could hardly speak.

"Rosa, you look like you're about to faint. Let me get you a glass of lemonade."

CHAPTER 7

"Why I Love America"

The blazing summer days crept by. Rosa fed the chickens in the morning and collected eggs. Mamá used them to give the family something other than beans to eat. Sometimes, she sold a few eggs to other families who no longer had chickens, or she sold them to the grocer in town. She used the money to buy flour and rice.

After Rosa came home from Mrs. Madden's house each afternoon, it was too hot to do anything except lie in the shade. Scorching heat made everyone sluggish, and sometimes Rosa would fall asleep under a tree with Isabella beside her. Her baby cousin was growing fast. No longer was she content to stay in her basket. She wanted to sit up and look around. Rosa tried to keep her cool with damp cloths.

At the end of August, the big day came. Rosa was so nervous she could hardly swallow her breakfast. The whole town would gather on Main Street and watch the ceremony as the three prize-winners read their essays. The third-place and second-place winners would go first. Then Rosa, first place, would read her essay.

Mamá and Papá were so proud. Rosa had translated her essay for them, and their faces beamed with pride. Rosa hoped that now they would understand why she wanted to get a good education in this new country. They all walked to town together that morning, even Tía. Rosa was worried that Tía was not well enough, but Tía said that nothing would keep her away, so Rosa might as well not try. She leaned heavily on Tío, and they had to walk slowly, but she kept going.

As they got close and Rosa saw the platform where the winners would sit, she almost turned around and ran home. She was proud of her essay, but to stand up in front of all those people and read it terrified her.

There was Henry! And Mrs. Madden! Rosa was so relieved to see them. Mrs. Madden gave her a great big hug and told her to breathe deeply and stand up straight. Rosa had every reason to be proud of herself, Mrs. Madden said. Rosa decided that she would look at Mrs. Madden in the crowd, and perhaps she would not be so nervous up on the stage. Her mind whirled so much that she hardly heard a word that the other prizewinners said. Then the mayor called for her. "I am pleased to introduce our first-prize winner, Miss Rosa Sanchez."

Rosa stood up awkwardly and stepped forward to the microphone. In her hand, she held a smooth, fresh paper. She had written out a clean copy of her essay just last night. Mrs. Madden smiled at her, and Rosa could not help but smile back. She began to read:

" 'Why I Love America,' by Rosa Sanchez
"Love is a beautiful word. We use this word to express our affection for one another. We use this word when we are excited about doing something special. We use this word when we take care of a lovely little baby. Is it really a word to use when we want to say how we feel about America?

*"America. Just to say the word makes my heart swell up
with pride. America. Just to hear the word makes my future
shine bright. America, a word that gives me hope. America,
a place where my dreams can come true.*

*"George Washington, Thomas Jefferson, Benjamin
Franklin, and all the other people in the 1700s had a vision.
They had a vision for freedom, for opportunity, for happi-
ness, for respect, for a country where hard work pays off. Our
country has had many difficult moments in its history, even
war and injustice. But we learned from these lessons. We did
not give up on the vision. We did not give up on the dream.
We did not give up on the hard work it takes to build a
strong nation.*

*"I think the founding fathers would be pleased with
what America has become. I know I am. I love America
because America never gives up."*

The applause began immediately. When Rosa stepped forward
to bow to the audience, as Mrs. Madden had told her to do, she
saw Papá clapping the hardest of all. Rosa grinned in relief as she
turned to the mayor and he hung a blue ribbon around her neck.

After the ceremony and after her family congratulated her again,
Rosa looked through the crowd to find Mrs. Madden once more.
She seemed to have disappeared, and Rosa thought perhaps she
had gone home already. Then she spotted Mrs. Madden's favorite
blue hat and ran toward it. As she got closer, her steps slowed. Mrs.
Madden was talking with a group of four or five people. Rosa recognized them. They were the school board.

"After a speech like that, how can you possibly justify sending the Mexican children to an inferior school?"

"But she's not even American," Mr. Elliot said. "Her family is Mexican."

"Her family came from Mexico, but Rosa was born right here in Dalhart. She is a citizen of the United States. Can you seriously listen to the words of that child and not see that in her heart she is as American as you and I? She deserves the same education that every other American child receives." Mrs. Madden looked flushed, even with a hat to shade her face.

Rosa held her breath as she waited for their response.

"I see that there is no dissuading you, Miz Madden," Mr. Decker said reluctantly.

"Absolutely not."

"We will take up the matter at our next regular board meeting," Mr. Orvid said.

"You'll take it up right now," Mrs. Madden insisted. "School begins soon. We don't have time to waste with school-board politics."

"Miz Madden, I will remind you of our service to the community," Mr. Elliot said. "If we kowtowed to every whim that someone brings to the board, we'd never make any progress in this town."

"We will never make any progress in this town until education is equally available to everyone who wants it. You're all here right now. Take a vote."

"This ain't the proper way to do things," Mr. Orvid protested.

"It's an efficient way," Mrs. Madden insisted.

Suddenly the sky rocked with thunder. Because of the dust, the sky often looked dreary. Rosa had not noticed the rain clouds roll in. As it began to rain, everyone's eyes turned to the sky.

"Rain! Rain!" Rather than seeking protection from the rain,

children—and even adults—began to dance in the drizzle. Gradually it became heavier and steadier. The morning festivities broke up with whooping and hollering as families raced to their homes to enjoy the rain.

"We've had five inches of rain this year," Tío pointed out at the end of the summer as he and Papá leaned against the fence and looked out at the field. Rosa could hear them easily from under the tree where she was sitting.

"Yes, but we should have had eighteen inches."

"Perhaps there is enough moisture in the ground to plant winter wheat. I hear some of the other farmers talking about that."

"Perhaps."

Rosa did not think Papá sounded convinced he should plant a winter crop. A couple of heavy rains made some people think the drought was over. The women talked about it in the shops in town. Even Mrs. Madden talked about it. Her husband was a minister, and many of the families in the church were suffering. He wanted to help them, but he did not know what he could do. He could not clap his hands and make it rain or wave his arms and make the grass grow for the cattle to eat. Mrs. Madden kept their home tidy and cozy, but they had very little money themselves.

As Papá and Tío drifted toward the house, Rosa stayed under the tree, thinking.

Rosa could hardly wait for the first day of school. Mrs. Madden had been successful in her crusade for equal education. Some of the parents of white children were unhappy with her, and they did not keep their feelings a secret. Someone had thrown a rock through a window of her house.

Rosa felt terrible about that. What if Henry had gotten hurt? Surely that would never have happened if Mrs. Madden had not started helping Rosa. If Rosa had been at her own school that day last spring, she would never have met Mrs. Madden, and none of this would have happened.

But Mrs. Madden was not frightened or worried. She told Rosa over and over that they were doing the right thing. Even Reverend Madden thought so. He preached in his church about justice and fairness.

Although she was eager to return to school, Rosa was nervous. What would it be like? What if she had not studied hard enough with Mrs. Madden? What about the other Mexican children who did not have anyone helping them? Would the white teachers want to teach the Mexican children?

Rosa spent the last days of summer going around to the homes of other Mexican families. She wanted to be sure that everyone understood that the children would now all go to school together. If some of the Mexican children were scared, she said to them, "How brave can you be?"

When the first day of school came, Rosa walked proudly to the school that held all the books and maps and teachers. No one would work as hard as she would. She wanted to learn everything!

CHAPTER 8

Sixth Grade

Rosa liked Mrs. Briggs immediately. As the class filed into the fifth- and sixth-grade room, Mrs. Briggs welcomed each student with a bright smile and a handshake. Two other Mexican children were assigned to Mrs. Briggs's room with Rosa. Miguel and Beatriz were in the fifth-grade section of the class.

They wanted to sit by themselves at the back of the class, but Mrs. Briggs pleasantly asked them to take seats near the front. She made sure that Miguel was next to a friendly boy and Beatriz was next to a friendly girl. Mrs. Briggs assigned Rosa a seat next to a girl named Sally Furman. Rosa had seen Sally in some of the shops in town, but they had never spoken to each other before. She smiled shyly at Sally, but Sally did not smile back.

By the end of the first week of school, Rosa was exhausted. Her worst fears had come true. She was not ready for sixth grade in this school. Her English was not as good as she wished, and she struggled to read and write as quickly as the other children. Rosa dreaded to think what school would be like if she had not studied with Mrs. Madden all summer.

By the end of the second week, the principal and the teacher agreed that Miguel and Beatriz would be better off if they joined the fourth-grade class. They were not quite ready for fifth-grade work. Rosa, however, was a hard worker. Anyone could see that. If she wanted to stay in the sixth grade, they would allow it. But she would have to be prepared to work harder than any other student. Rosa quickly agreed. She wanted to keep moving forward, not step back to the fifth grade.

Now Rosa was the only Mexican student in Mrs. Briggs's room. As she studied her books and worked on her papers, she felt the eyes of the other students on her. She also heard them talking on the playground, so she knew that many of them wanted her to leave their class. Their parents, they said, were going to make the school board change things back to the way they were before. Some of them said they were going to stop going to Reverend Madden's church.

Mrs. Madden assured Rosa that the Mexican children were in school to stay. She and Reverend Madden were prepared to insist on equal education even if the rest of the town objected. With enough time, Mrs. Madden said, everyone would accept the new ways. In the meantime, Rosa just had to focus on her schoolwork and not pay any attention to what the other students said.

Rosa resumed going to Mrs. Madden's home after school for extra lessons. Sometimes she asked for help with her homework when it was too hard for her to do alone. The multiplication and division problems that Mrs. Briggs gave the class were harder than anything Rosa had ever done, and she had never studied fractions before. Rosa was determined to succeed in sixth grade. In fact, she wanted to be the best student in Mrs. Briggs's class. Every night, she took books home to study. She sat at a little desk in her bedroom where no one would disturb her.

The late summer days turned into fall days. The fall days grew brisk, then nippy, then cold. Rosa wrapped herself in the warmest clothes she could find. She had outgrown most of her clothes, and Mamá could not afford cloth to make new ones. Rosa tried not to care that she only had two dresses left and one of them was getting too short.

Winter blasted into the panhandle of Texas just in time for the Christmas break from school. The temperature was below zero on many days. Sometimes it was hard for Rosa to remember what it was like when the temperature was over one hundred degrees. *Somewhere in between zero and one hundred would be much better,* she thought.

On the last day of school before Christmas, Mrs. Briggs handed out report cards. The Mexican school never had report cards. Rosa was not sure she wanted to look at hers. What if her grades were all Ds? Would they make her go back to fifth grade? She carried the envelope with her as she scuffed her way down the street to Mrs. Madden's house. Without speaking, she handed it to Mrs. Madden, who opened it. Rosa watched her face carefully.

"Why, Rosa, this is a report card you can be very proud of." Mrs. Madden beamed.

"Really?"

"Really. Look for yourself." She handed the card back to Rosa.

Reading: B. Spelling: A. Math: B. Social Studies: A. Science: A. Writing: B. Mrs. Briggs even wrote a note at the bottom that said, "Rosa is a pleasure to have in our class. She makes wonderful contributions to our class discussions."

Rosa gave a big sigh of relief.

That night, Rosa's brothers told her stories of the Christmas parties and decorations and foods they had enjoyed in Mexico. On

December 16, the first parade of candlelight happened. The children walked through the village with candles every afternoon for nine days. Each day, Mexican children made up a play about Mary and Joseph searching for a place to stay in Bethlehem so Jesus could be born there. Sometimes Mary, the *Virgen Maria*, rode on a burro and Joseph, *San José*, led the burro. Other children played the angels and shepherds. Everyone wore a colorful costume and carried paper lanterns. After the play came the party with piñatas full of fruit, sugarcane, peanuts, and candy.

In Mexico, all the aunts and uncles and cousins went to church together on Christmas Eve and then shared a huge meal of tamales and corn gruel. When everyone was full, they opened their gifts to each other and played until the wee hours of the morning.

Rosa's family had a much simpler celebration in Texas. But they did bring some traditions from Mexico. Mamá always put out the *El Nacimiento*, clay pieces arranged in a stable. Mamá had Mary, Joseph, baby Jesus, three shepherds, an ox, and two sheep. Rosa loved to play with the pieces and tell the story over and over. She did not mind that there were no *Las Posadas* parades or piñata parties. Rosa was happy just being with her family at Christmastime, especially since little Isabella was born. But she did wonder about one thing.

"Why don't we go to church here?" Rosa asked one day as the family ate supper.

Papá took a bite of his beans. "It is not the same here. The churches are different. I do not think they want us."

"But, Papá," Rosa protested, "don't we still believe in God?"

"Yes, Rosita, we believe in God. But it is not the same. You are too young to understand."

"I want to go to church," Rosa insisted. "We can go to Reverend Madden's church. They have a service on Christmas Eve, just like in Mexico."

"We can have church here, if you like," Papá said. "You can use the El Nacimiento and tell us the story of how Jesus was born."

"No, Papá, I want to go to church!" Rosa repeated. "I want to go to Mrs. Madden's church on Christmas Eve."

Papá looked at Mamá. Mamá shrugged.

"Okay, Rosita," Papá said. "We will go to church."

Rosa imagined what Christmas Eve at church would be like. She dreamed of candles and music and crowds of people. *I wish I had a pretty dress to wear,* Rosa thought. But she knew Mamá would not be able to give her a new dress, so she did not ask for one.

Christmas Eve finally came. The whole family cleaned up and put on their best clothes and their warmest coats. Rosa wore her brown dress. It only had one small patch. Even Tía got ready for church. Without the summer dust storms, she felt much better. Rosa held Papá's hand and led the way into town. Papá carried a lantern so they could see the road in the dark. Rosa knew right where to go and wanted to be early so they could sit up front.

Across the church, Mrs. Madden held a sleeping Henry while Rosa held a sleeping Isabella. They smiled at each other. Mamá and Papá did not know all the English words to the Christmas songs, but Rosa heard them humming the tunes. Rosa used a hymnal and followed the words to each song with a finger.

At home again after church, Rosa's family opened their gifts. The presents were simple. Papá had done some carpentry work for the grocer in town in exchange for some large oranges. Mamá used some precious flour and sugar to make cookies. When Tía handed

Rosa a package wrapped in burlap, Rosa looked up in surprise.

"You have been a great help with the baby," Tía said. "This gift is to thank you." She smiled gently at Rosa.

"But I love Isabella," Rosa said. "I love taking care of her."

"I still want to say thank you."

Rosa opened the burlap package and gasped. Tía had cut down another one of her favorite dresses to fit Rosa. Rosa lifted it out of the package, stood up, and held it against herself. "Tía! Thank you! It's beautiful! But I know this was your favorite."

"You are my favorite, Rosita. This is just a dress."

"And now it is time for tamales and rice," Mamá said. She stood up and kissed the top of Rosa's head before going to the kitchen to cook.

Everyone stayed up very late, just like in Mexico. Rosa fell asleep on the floor clutching her new dress, and her brother Téodoro carried her up to her bed. She woke only when he bent over and kissed her forehead. "*Feliz Navidad*, Rosita," he said, and Rosa smiled her way back to sleep. "Merry Christmas."

Rosa woke after a long sleep. The sun was already high in the sky. She had slept away half the morning. She smiled again as she saw her new dress laid across the end of her bed. This was Christmas Day!

But something did not feel right.

Rosa got up and dressed and headed down the stairs toward the kitchen. She walked quietly, not wanting anyone to hear her. At the bottom of the stairs, she sat and listened to her parents.

Mamá was crying. Why was Mamá crying?

"We knew he wanted to go," Papá said. "He is a man now. He makes his own choices."

"Just because he is a man does not mean he must break his mother's heart," Mamá responded between sobs.

Gone? Rosa realized Mamá and Papá were talking about Téodoro. That's why he had carried her to bed and kissed her head. Téodoro had been planning to leave, and now he had left! Rosa jumped off the step and ran into the kitchen.

"Where is he?" she cried. "Where is Téodoro?"

Mamá looked up from her tears.

"How could he leave us?" Rosa demanded.

Papá opened his arms to hold Rosa. "He has made his decision," he said. "Téodoro left during the night. He has been talking of nothing but California for weeks. He decided it was time to go."

"But we stick together. We help each other."

Papá nodded. "Téodoro believes he can help from California. He will pick fruit and send money home."

Rosa was silent, her head on her father's shoulder. After a moment, she asked, "Will we ever see Téodoro again?"

CHAPTER 9

Then Came Spring

Rosa strode toward home with confidence. She loved being in the sixth grade! She was a good speller and had learned to read English words smoothly. Fractions no longer frightened her. Rosa worked hard and was proud of being a good student.

As she approached the road turning toward her home, her steps slowed. It was her job to stop at the end of the road every day and check the mailbox. She used to be excited about doing that job, wondering every day what might come. But now, she wished she did not have to do it. Every day, Mamá hoped there would be a letter from Téodoro. And every day, no letter came. Téodoro had been gone almost three months, and the family had not heard from him. Mamá's sadness made her look older than she really was.

Winter was on its way out, and spring on its way in. Soon Papá and Tío would decide whether to try to plant any crops. They would go out on the range and count how many cattle had survived the winter. Usually Téodoro helped to find the cattle. Most years he found more than anyone else. Rafaél insisted that he could take Téodoro's place. *Perhaps he can do Téodoro's job,* Rosa thought, *but no one can take Téodoro's place.*

Rosa stopped at the mailbox just as she did every day. Empty.

Rosa thought, *At least I don't have to give Mamá a bill that we can't afford to pay.*

As Rosa climbed the steps in front of the house, Mamá came to the door and looked at her, hopefully. Rosa shook her head. "No, Mamá, nothing from Téodoro." Mamá nodded and turned around to go upstairs. Rosa knew Mamá would go to her bedroom to cry. Papá and Rafaél and Juan all missed Téodoro, but sometimes Rosa thought Mamá missed him most of all.

Rafaél was sixteen now. How much longer would he stay at home with the family? Juan was fifteen. He loved to take care of the animals, but every year they had fewer animals. Papá had sold the horses and one of the milk cows during the winter, and they could barely afford to feed a few chickens. If a hen stopped laying eggs, Mamá cooked it. The family could not afford to feed an animal that did not give them something back.

Rosa wished Mamá would cook more eggs for the family. Most of the time, Mamá sold the eggs for money she could use to buy other things they needed. The only pig they had left was going to have piglets soon, which gave Juan something to look forward to. Selling some of the piglets would bring in some money.

Rosa used to love spring. The season meant fresh air, planting vegetables, spring cleaning in the house, and knowing that long summer days would soon be here. The land was flat for mile after mile. The wheat grew taller than she was and swayed in the breeze, looking like a field of gold. When she was little, Rosa loved to run through the field, hiding from her brothers in the wheat while Papá watched and laughed at her games.

But this year, 1935, Rosa wished the winter weather would stay. Perhaps it would snow and bring more moisture to the ground.

Spring reminded the whole family that they had no crops. And spring meant that the dust storms would start again. Tía would get sick again. Isabella would cry for her mother, and she might get sick, too. Spring meant that summer would follow, hot summer days with no rain bringing relief. Rosa hated the dust storms.

One day Papá came home from town, and his face was glowing.

"*Hermano*," Tío said, "what are you so happy about?"

Rosa had not seen her father look so hopeful in a long time.

"I have learned more about the new project," Papá said. "The government is going to help with erosion control."

"What kind of project is this?" Tío asked.

"The Federal Land Bank has come to Texas. They have chosen our town for the demonstration project."

"What does that mean?" Rosa asked.

Papá explained. "A demonstration project shows everyone better ways to do something. This project will show us better ways to keep the soil from blowing away in the wind."

"But it's too late," Tío said. "The soil has been blowing away for years. There is nothing left."

"This project will show us how to rebuild the soil and keep it where it belongs," Papá said.

"Will it give us a crop this year?" Tío asked. "Will it grow grass for the cattle to eat?"

Papá shook his head slowly. "No, not this year. But maybe next year."

"Next year is a long time to wait," Tío said.

"Perhaps it will rain this year," Papá said. "Perhaps God will send the rain and keep us together one more year."

Rosa thought about all the times that Tío was the one to say that rain would come and they would have a crop again. Now even Tío didn't think it could happen.

The wind began to blow the next day. Rosa felt the familiar taste of dirt in her mouth while she sat at her desk in school. The day was stifling, and the windows were open. Mrs. Briggs continued her lecture about Texas history as she closed one window after another. Rosa groaned inwardly. Now the room would become even hotter. Closing the windows might keep out some of the dust, but it did not keep out the howl of the wind. Rosa gazed through the rattling glass, discouraged at the thought of another summer like last year's.

At home, Mamá would be running around trying to cover furniture with old sheets, while Tía would be making sure everything in the kitchen was closed up. But Rosa knew nothing would help. The wind would blow, and the dirt would fly through the air and land wherever it wanted to. Mamá and Tía could do nothing to stop it, any more than Papá could make the dry, thin soil grow a crop.

"Why doesn't God send us some rain?" Rosa asked Mrs. Madden one day after school. "You told me the story about Noah, when too much rain fell and the world was flooded. Why can't we have some of that rain now?"

Mrs. Madden sighed. "We can't always understand the ways of God, Rosa," she said. "That doesn't mean He's not taking care of us. He gives us what we need at just the right time."

Rosa was thoughtful. "What if He forgets?"

"God doesn't forget, Rosa."

"Is He taking care of Téodoro?" Rosa asked.

"I'm sure He is."

"I wish He would tell Téodoro to write Mamá a letter."

"Perhaps He will. You must not give up hope. We must never give up hope."

"Ope," little Henry said. "Osa ope."

Rosa laughed. "Yes, Henry, I will hope." She scooped him up in her arms and tickled his belly.

Mrs. Madden laughed, too, and took Henry from Rosa's arms. "Time for you to get back to your lesson, young lady."

Rosa turned back to her book. *We may not have any rain,* she thought, *but at least I still have school and my lessons with Mrs. Madden.*

Isabella had begun to walk. Now Rosa followed her little cousin around making sure she was safe. Isabella was a curious little girl. She loved to touch everything and climb on anything she could. Rosa held her little hand and took her for walks down the road. When Isabella was tired, Rosa carried her home and laid her down for a nap.

Isabella did not understand what a drought was. She did not know there would be no crop this year. She did not know that the animals on the range had nothing to eat. She simply loved to explore her world and learn everything about it.

Rosa wished that she could feel that way again. She wished she did not have to see the worry lines in Papá's face or the way

Tío looked at Tía to see if she was going to start coughing. Rosa wished she did not have to see the sadness in Mamá's eyes when no letter came from Téodoro day after day.

One day when Rosa came home from school, Mamá was ripping up the old sheets and had a stack of burlap sacks.

"What are you doing, Mamá?" Rosa asked.

"It makes no sense to cover the furniture when the dust still comes in and makes us sick."

"So what are we going to do?"

"You can help me stuff these rags into the cracks around the windows and doors so the dirt can't get in."

"Do you really think that will help?" Rosa asked as she picked up a burlap sack. "We've done that before, and the dust still comes in."

"We have to try something," Mamá said. "We will use every inch of extra fabric we can find. I am tired of living in a filthy house." Mamá ripped a long strip off a sheet. "Soon we will all be as sick as your tía."

Rosa worked all afternoon, stuffing rags, towels, and old clothing into any open space she could find. Standing on a chair, she reached above the back door to feel for air coming in. Dust immediately left a thick coat on her fingers. Rosa used a wet rag to wipe the dirt away, then stuffed a strip of a sheet into the space. Mamá pushed furniture out of the way so she could reach the windows. Rosa handed her one rag after another.

Isabella toddled around after them, pointing at windows.

"Window," Rosa said clearly for the child. She made sure to teach Isabella the English words for the things she pointed at. Everyone else would teach her the Spanish words.

Rosa hated the dust and dirt, but she also dreaded having

to keep the windows closed all the time. The house would get so hot!

The next day when Rosa got home, Mamá and Tía were hanging the wash on a line in the backyard. Rosa went into the kitchen and saw the large kettle of boiling water. She knew that Mamá had been scrubbing clothes on a washboard all day, then swishing them around in the boiling water. Spring days were cool, so it was not so bad standing over the hot water. Soon summer would arrive, and the days would be hot. Rosa hated to think about Mamá and Tía working so hard in a hot kitchen. She wanted to keep up with her studies with Mrs. Madden in the summer, but she promised herself that she would work harder to help Mamá at home, too.

The winds blew and blew. Everyone in Rosa's family grew more quiet each day. They all knew what the winds meant. They would have another hard year, another summer with not enough rain, another season with no crop to harvest, another year without money.

As she hung wash in the yard, Mamá often gazed toward the western horizon. Rosa wished she could go find Téodoro and bring him home. What if he never wrote a letter? What if he never came home? What if she never saw her brother again? No wonder Mamá felt so sad.

At bedtime, Rosa helped Tía get Isabella settled down for the night. She was getting too big for her basket, but Tía still wanted Isabella to sleep there. It was easier to keep the dust off of her that way.

Every night before Rosa went to bed, she ran some cool water on a washcloth. She lay straight on her back and put the damp cloth over her face to keep the dirt out of her nose and mouth. If she didn't keep perfectly still all night, the washcloth fell off and she woke up with her mouth full of dirt.

Rosa hated the dust storms.

CHAPTER 10

Creak and *Crash!*

"But, Mamá, it's a flour sack!" Rosa protested.

Mamá held the sack up against Rosa to see if it was long enough for a blouse.

"Mamá, you can't use a flour sack to make me clothes."

"Unless you can make yourself stop growing, you need new clothes. I have no fabric, Rosita, no money to buy any, and no more old dresses I can cut down for you."

"I won't wear a flour sack!" Rosa insisted. She pushed her mother's arms away from her.

"Would you rather have a burlap sack?"

Rosa was horrified. "You wouldn't really make me wear burlap, would you?"

"You can choose. Burlap or the cotton fabric of a flour sack."

Rosa sighed and could hardly keep herself from crying. "Please make sure the writing doesn't show," she finally said.

Mamá softened. "Oh, mi hija, I don't like this, either. But what choice do I have?" She brightened. "Perhaps we can dye the fabric. You can choose a color."

Rosa raised her eyes to her mother's but said nothing.

"I still have a few beets in their juice in the cellar," Mamá said. "Or we can look for some wildflowers."

"Beet juice will not make a flour sack pretty, Mamá."

"I'm sorry, hija. I don't know what else to do."

Rosa did not want to be the first student in her class to wear clothes made out of flour sacks. She promised herself she would only wear the flour sack blouse at home. School was almost out for the year. For the summer lessons, Mrs. Madden would understand—she hoped.

Rosa was determined to make her report card at the end of sixth grade the best she could do. She had passed most of the other students in the class. No one wanted to be friends with a Mexican girl who was smart, however, so Rosa was lonely. Even Sally, who sat right next to her, ignored her when she saw Rosa earning one A after another. Rosa sat at lunch by herself and played at recess by herself.

Rosa didn't want to play, anyway. Instead of going outside for lunch and recess, Rosa asked Mrs. Briggs for extra lessons. After that, the other students called her the teacher's pet. But Rosa didn't care. It was more important to learn everything she could than to have lots of friends. She told herself it didn't matter. One day, she would finish school and become a teacher herself. Then she would have all the friends she needed.

In the meantime, she had Mamá and Papá, and Tío and Tía, and Rafaél and Juan, and Mrs. Madden. And somewhere in California, she had Téodoro. She hoped he thought about all of them as much as they thought about him.

Mrs. Briggs began to tell the other teachers what a hardworking student Rosa was. While Rosa sat outside eating lunch by herself one day, the second-grade teacher came and sat beside her.

"Are you Rosa?" the teacher asked.

"Yes, ma'am," Rosa answered, wondering what this teacher wanted. For a moment, she was afraid they were going to send her back to second grade.

"My name is Miss Cordray," the teacher said. "I teach first and second grade. I have some students who need some extra help. Mrs. Briggs thinks you might be just the person to help them."

"Me?"

Miss Cordray smiled. "Yes, you. Mrs. Briggs tells me that you are bright and hardworking. She thinks you would be patient with the younger children."

"I help take care of my cousin, Isabella, and Mrs. Madden's son, Henry. They're not old enough for school."

"That's excellent experience," Miss Cordray said with a smile. "Would you like to meet your new students?"

Rosa's eyes widened in excitement. "You mean today—right now?"

"Certainly. I'll introduce you today, and tomorrow you can begin helping them with their lessons at lunchtime. Would you like to do that?"

"Yes, yes, yes!" Rosa exclaimed. She followed Miss Cordray into the building and met Jeannie, Sylvia, and Marcos. Each day, she would work with a different student on spelling and simple arithmetic. She would also listen to them read and help them figure out how to say the hard words.

Rosa ran to Mrs. Madden's house after school with the good news. "I'm going to be a teacher! I'm going to be a teacher!"

Mrs. Madden gave Rosa a great big hug. "I knew you could do it, Rosa. You can do anything you put your mind to."

Henry reached up for Rosa. "Hope. Hope."

Rosa laughed. "Yes, Henry, I still have hope. I will keep hoping." She picked him up under his arms and twirled him around.

Rosa loved helping the younger students. Helping them learn was almost as much fun as learning herself! Jeannie was writing some of her letters backward. She made a *b* look like a *d*. Rosa guided her hand over and over as Jeannie practiced the hard letters as well as the easy ones. Soon they moved on to writing whole words, then sentences.

Sylvia was having trouble with subtraction. She would add well, but she did not understand that subtraction was the opposite of adding. Rosa gave her real problems to figure out.

"If my hen lays four eggs and your hen lays seven eggs, how many eggs do we have together?" she asked. Then, "The crate had twelve eggs in the morning. In the afternoon, I count only eight. How many are gone?"

The words helped more than just looking at numbers on a chalkboard, and soon Sylvia was more confident.

Marcos was a smart little boy. He just needed some help with his English, and Rosa was glad to help him. No one at his house ever spoke any English words to him. When he started second grade, he did not know how to say anything in English. Rosa loved to speak English with another Mexican child. She was patient while he figured out what she was talking about. When he started to ask questions in Spanish, she made him use English. She was sure that by the time he started third grade, he would be doing very well.

By the middle of April, many of the children were eager for school to be out for the summer. They were ready to set their books aside and run free. Rosa kept working hard in her own class and helping the second graders at lunchtime. She could hear the other students on the playground, and she knew it was hard for Jeannie, Sylvia, and Marcos to stay inside and work, so she tried to make it as fun as she could. She asked them riddles while they ate their lunch before they got down to work.

On Thursdays, it was Sylvia's turn to be inside with Rosa. Sylvia stood at the chalkboard, and Rosa sat at a desk nearby. Rosa made up math problems, and Sylvia listened for clues about what numbers to write on the board. Then she figured out the answer, and Rosa cheered for her. Rosa tried to be quiet while Sylvia was thinking. The sounds from the playground wafted through the window, but the only other sound was Sylvia's chalk clicking against the chalkboard. So when Rosa heard a creaking sound, she jumped up immediately.

"What is it?" Sylvia wanted to know. "Did I make a mistake?"

"*Shh,*" Rosa answered in a whisper. "You're doing fine. Just listen."

They both stood perfectly still, listening, hardly daring to breathe. There it was again! Something was creaking. Rosa began to feel funny. Something was wrong.

"Sylvia, we have to get out of here!" Rosa exclaimed.

"But I haven't solved the problem yet," Sylvia protested.

"Don't worry about that. We have to get out of here."

"Why? I don't want to go. Having lessons with you is fun. I want to stay here." Sylvia stuck out her lower lip in a pout.

Rosa heard the *creak* again, this time louder. She looked up and saw a crack beginning in the ceiling. Sylvia would have to do her pouting outside.

"We have to go now!" Rosa shouted. She grabbed Sylvia's shoulder and dragged her out of the classroom.

"I didn't finish my lunch," Sylvia whined, trying to turn around. "Miss Cordray won't let me eat during class."

"Sylvia, run!" Rosa commanded, pulling on the little girl's arm. They dashed down the hallway. The third- and fourth-grade class was next door to the second-grade room. Rosa ran past, then stopped abruptly.

"There's someone in there," she said to Sylvia. "You run outside. Don't wait for me."

"I'm scared, Rosa!" Sylvia said. "Stay with me!"

"Go!" Rosa screamed. She shoved Sylvia toward the door.

Rosa ran into the third- and fourth-grade room and saw the teacher with a student.

"The ceiling is falling in!" Rosa exclaimed.

The teacher made a face at her. "Don't be silly."

Then the ceiling creaked again. The teacher jumped up. She heard it, too!

"We have to get out!" Rosa insisted.

The teacher grabbed her student's hand, and the three of them ran down the hall and out the door as the *creak* became a *crash!* Once they were outside, Rosa turned around and looked at the school building. A swirl of dust exploded into a cloud as the ceiling fell into the first classroom. The third- and fourth-grade room was next. Teachers came running out of their rooms, and the principal came out of her office. Teachers and students stood on the playground and watched as the two classrooms collapsed.

"Is everyone out? Is everyone out?" The principal rushed around the playground looking for any missing children. "Have you all found your brothers and sisters?"

"Rosa! Rosa!" Miss Cordray called, her voice rising above the noise of the gathering crowd.

"I'm here!" Rosa shouted, turning toward Miss Cordray's voice. "Sylvia is fine. We're both here!"

"Oh, thank goodness," Miss Cordray said when she found them. "When I saw the roof start to fall in—I didn't want to think what might happen to you."

"Rosa heard a *creak*," Sylvia announced. "Rosa told me I had to get out. She made me. She pushed me."

"You did exactly the right thing," Miss Cordray said.

"Then she went in the third- and fourth-grade room," Sylvia continued. "She got people out of there, too."

By now, Mrs. Briggs had found Rosa, as well. The principal had made certain no one else was in the building. Townspeople gathered and gawked at the school with the big hole in the roof.

"It's the dirt," Mrs. Briggs said to Rosa. "The dirt from last year's dust storms was never cleared away, and this year's dirt has made it worse. The principal kept telling the school board they had to do something. Now that the storms have started again, the weight was too much for the roof."

"I never thought that dirt could make a roof cave in," Rosa murmured.

"Now the school will have to close," Mrs. Briggs said sadly. "The city inspector will never let us take children back into that building."

"But we still have six weeks of school left to go."

Mrs. Briggs shook her head sadly. "I think we're finished for the year, Rosa."

"Will they fix the building over the summer?"

"I don't know."

Rosa held back the tears trying to escape her eyes. She had finally gotten to go to a real school, and now the school was turning into a pile of rubble.

She hated the dust storms!

CHAPTER 11

Black Sunday

"Please, Papá?" Rosa asked. "Please come to church with me tonight." Rosa had begun walking into town to attend the Maddens' church on Sundays. The church had a service at ten o'clock in the morning and another one at six o'clock in the evening. Rosa liked to go to both of them because she loved to hear the singing.

"Rosita, you know I am not comfortable with the ways of this church."

"But Papá, Reverend and Mrs. Madden are so nice, and they always ask me how you are."

"I hope that you tell them that I am fine."

"Yes, I do, but it would be so nice for them to see you."

Papá sighed. "I will think about it. Ask me again when you are ready to leave."

Rosa was hopeful all afternoon that Papá would go with her to church. And if Papá went, maybe Mamá would come, too. *She would like the singing,* Rosa thought.

Mamá had spent Saturday digging up the remains of last year's failed garden. She thought she might get some potatoes and onions to grow this year. Mamá's garden shovel was still in front of the house. Rosa was supposed to put it away yesterday, but she did not want to walk all the way to the barn. Instead, she had kicked it next to the porch and hoped Mamá would not see it there.

The sky had been blue all day with no breeze. It was April 14, and after the storm at the end of March that destroyed so much land, everyone was glad to be able to go outside and enjoy a nice day. A beautiful afternoon made people want to go on a picnic or take a nap in the sun. Rosa took Isabella for a walk down the road, and then they came back to the house and lay down on a blanket in the sun. Both of them slept soundly. Rosa awoke only when Isabella began to climb on her and poke her nose.

"Isabella, you silly girl," Rosa said, tickling the baby's bare belly.

Isabella grinned at her cousin.

Rosa kissed Isabella's cheek. "Let's go see how your mamá is feeling."

At five o'clock that afternoon, Rosa was ready to go to church. But where was Papá? She looked in every room in the house but could not find him. *He thinks I will give up on looking for him,* Rosa thought, *but I won't. He's going to come to church with me.*

Rosa went outside and looked in the barn, calling for her father. He did not answer. She finally had to admit that he must have gone out to one of the fields. He could be anywhere. If she went to look for him, she would be late for church. Rosa sighed. She would have to go without him and ask him again next week.

Rosa scanned the sky and noticed that the afternoon had turned cool. It seemed to get colder by the moment. Rosa decided she should take her jacket to church with her in case it was even colder after the service.

When she came back out of the house with her jacket, Rosa looked up at the trees. Lots of birds made their home on the ranch and around the house. Usually Rosa saw only a few at a time, and they were so quiet she did not know what sound they made. Now the birds were making a clatter, as if they were chattering to each other and telling important news. More and more birds flew in and joined in the discussion. Rosa told herself to remember to ask Mrs. Madden if she knew why the birds would suddenly start making so much noise.

Rosa started down the road toward town, humming some of the songs she had learned at church. She waved at people who drove by in their cars. Some of them were men who worked on other parts of the large ranch where the Sanchez family lived. They recognized Rosa and waved back.

Suddenly the birds stopped chattering and began to flap their wings instead. Hordes of birds took off and flew away, all in one direction. Rosa had never seen so many birds flying at one time. This was another question for Mrs. Madden.

A huge black cloud stirred on the horizon. Rosa hugged her jacket around her. The cloud raced toward town. The temperature was dropping rapidly. Maybe it would rain! Maybe that's what Papá was doing out in the fields—waiting for rain.

She looked again at the cloud, and her heart sank. It was not a rain cloud. It was a dust cloud, and it was coming fast. Hadn't they just had a major dust storm two weeks ago? The dirt from that storm had ruined the school and many of the houses in town. That was enough damage. Was such a beautiful day going to turn into a terrible storm?

Rosa stood on the side of the street, unsure what to do. She wanted to go to church, but if the black cloud was bringing a dust storm, she knew she should go home as quickly as possible. She had to find shelter.

A moment later, Rosa knew she had no choice but to turn around and race home as fast as she could. This was the worst storm she had ever seen! Even though the sun was still shining, the air had become black as midnight. Rosa hated all dust storms, but this one was frightening. Before Rosa could turn around, the wind rushed down, nearly knocking her off balance. Around her, cars picked up speed. Everyone was racing home before the worst of the storm hit.

Rosa could no longer see the sun. As black dust filled the air, it was hard to see the fences and trees or to see where she was going. She could hardly keep her eyes open for one second at a time without getting dirt in them. One step at a time, Rosa felt for the side of the road with her foot. If she could just stay on the road, she would make it home. She had not gone very far down the road when the cloud descended and swirled around her. If she only had a light! She might at least be able to see right in front of her face.

Cars whizzed by. Rosa could hardly stand up any longer because the wind was so strong. In the dark, she was afraid that drivers would not be able to see her on the side of the road. She stepped to the shoulder. Even though cars had headlights on, Rosa could not see them coming toward her until they were right in front of her. And the wind was howling so hard that she did not hear the cars until they were right next to her. Because of the roar of the wind, when one of the cars stopped, Rosa did not realize it. Every few steps, she would feel for the side of the road to be sure she had not wandered off to get lost in the dark.

Suddenly the strong arms of a man wrapped around Rosa and scooped her up, just the way she scooped up Henry or Isabella.

Rosa screamed, and her mouth filled with dirt. The person who carried her opened a car door and dumped Rosa onto the backseat. Who was taking her? Where were they taking her? She just wanted to go home and find Papá.

Inside the car, Rosa opened her eyes and sputtered to get the dirt out of her mouth. Dirt was coming in even through the cracks in the door, and a mound of dirt had blown in while the car door was open. She looked to see who was in the front seat.

"Oh, *Señor* Garcia, thank you! I didn't hear your car coming." Señor Garcia worked with Papá on the ranch.

Señor Garcia pulled out on the road again. "What are you doing out in the middle of this storm, Rosa?"

"I wanted to go to church. The storm had not started yet when I left."

Señor Garcia nodded. "Yes, it came up suddenly. But you would never have made it home. I'm not sure I'll make it home even in a car."

The roadway was filling with drifts of dirt. Swirling wind made it almost impossible to see well enough to drive. Cars slowed down to a crawl, but drivers kept going. They knew if they stayed in one place, their cars would soon be buried.

"Help me find your road, Rosa," Mr. Garcia said.

Rosa hunched forward and looked out the front of the car. She hardly recognized anything that she saw. It was all shadows and blackness.

"There!" she said suddenly, as she pointed. "It's right there!"

Señor Garcia made the turn and drove as close to the house as he could get.

"Maybe you should come inside, Señor Garcia," Rosa suggested.

He shook his head. "No, I must get home to my family. They will be worried."

"Thank you for stopping to pick me up."

"You just get inside the house and stay there." Señor Garcia reached behind him and pushed open the car door. "Go!"

Rosa squeezed her eyes against the dust and covered her mouth with the edge of her jacket. She ran as fast as she could, although she was not sure where the door was. When she tripped on the front steps, she knew she was close. Rosa put her hands out in front of her and felt for the door. With relief she found the doorknob and turned it. Inside, she pushed the door closed again and leaned against it, trying to catch her breath.

"Rosita!" Mamá called. "I was frightened for you."

"I'm okay, Mamá," Rosa said as she fell into her mother's arms. "Señor Garcia found me and brought me home." Rosa looked around. "Where is Papá? I couldn't find him when I left for church."

Mamá shook her head. "He went out on the range hours ago. He has not come home."

"Papá is out in this storm?"

Mamá nodded silently.

"We have to find him, Mamá!"

"No, Rosita. I want your papá to come home as much as you do, but it is too dangerous to go out and look for him."

"We can't just stay here."

"We have no choice, Rosa. Your father would not want any of us to be in danger. We must stay in the house."

Rosa looked into the faces of Rafaél and Juan. Their eyes told her that they agreed with Mamá.

"What about Tío? He could go."

"No, Rosita. You must listen to me. I would not ask Tío to do something so dangerous."

"But Mamá—"

"No, Rosita. No more. We all know what these storms can do. We will wait. If you want to do something for your papá, you can pray." Mamá turned around and walked into the kitchen. Rosa heard the sound of pots banging against the stove. She could not believe Mamá was thinking about cooking in the middle of this storm.

Rosa moved to a window and looked out. She could see nothing. Everything was black.

"Do you really think Papá needs you to take care of him?" Juan asked in a mocking way.

"Listen to Mamá," Rafaél said. "You did not go to church, but if you really believe in God, you can pray for Papá here."

Rosa stuck her tongue out at her brothers as they left the room.

Rosa stood at the window trying to pray. But she was too frightened for Papá. She had to do something. Rosa looked around the room once again to be sure no one had returned.

Then she opened the front door and threw herself into the wind.

CHAPTER 12

Follow the Fence

Just as she closed the front door, Rosa heard her mother's footsteps coming across the living room. Rosa did not look back. Instead, she leapt off the porch and headed for the barn. The storm still raged.

If she could just get to the barn, she could find a lantern. She knew right where it was hanging, just inside the door. But where was the barn? Outside in the blackness, it was hard to know which direction to go. When she heard the frightened hens clacking inside the henhouse, Rosa knew she was close to the barn. Now she knew her way, and in a few minutes she was inside the barn and taking the lantern off its hook.

She groped in the darkness for the matches that Papá kept on a little ledge next to the hook. In the dark, she lit the lantern. Rosa had to try four times before the match burst with flame. She slipped the matches in her pocket and steeled herself to go back outside. It seemed like such a small light compared to the huge blackness.

She was going to find Papá.

Sunday morning seemed so long ago, not just twelve hours ago. Rosa had been sleepy and was late to breakfast. Papá had scowled at her and then kissed her cheek.

As she bent into the black wind, Rosa remembered what Papá and Tío had talked about at breakfast.

"The last storm did some damage on the north end of the pasture," Tío told Papá. "We will have to raise some fence posts, or the next storm will bury the fence."

"I'll go out and look," Papá answered. "We should fix the fences before we have another storm."

Tío nodded as he sipped his coffee. "I will do it soon."

Papá shook his head. "No, you stay with your wife. She is still ill from the last storm. I will look at the fences."

Rosa knew where to find her papá. But could she get there safely? She glanced back at the house and saw a light in a window. The house seemed so far away. But Rosa had a plan. She could find the beginning of the fence that went to the north end of the pasture. As long as she kept one hand on the fence, she would not get lost. When the wind blew hard, she would hold on to the fence with two hands. Maybe Papá would see the light and know that someone was coming to help him.

But what if Papá was already hurt? Rosa did not want to think about that.

The fence began as a wooden fence. Rosa had no trouble feeling it. After awhile, however, the fence changed to wires connected to wooden fence posts. And the wires had barbs on them. Barbed wire was supposed to keep cattle thieves out and to keep the best cows from wandering too far. Usually Rosa paid no attention to it. Today, though, she paid attention to every inch. She knew the barbs would cut her hands. In her mind, she tried to imagine how far apart the barbs were. When she got close to one, she raised her hand, but the barbs were too close together. In only a few minutes, Rosa's hands were cut and bleeding. But she didn't care. She kept going.

"Papá! Papá!"

The only answer Rosa heard was a howling wind.

I should have listened to Mamá, Rosa thought. *What if Papá is not in the pasture?* The house was getting farther and farther away. Rosa was not sure she could get back to the house safely, but she was not sure she could find Papá either.

Rosa kept going, calling for Papá. Her jacket was not enough to keep her warm, and she shivered in the wind. The fence cut her hands over and over, but she kept going. The dirt was piled up as high as her knees, and it was getting hard to walk. After only a few minutes, Rosa was so tired, she could hardly stand. "Papá!" she screamed. "Papá!"

Rosa sank to the ground, coughing, trying to get a clear breath. *What would Mrs. Madden do?* Rosa thought. She knew the answer. Mrs. Madden would believe that God would take care of her, and she would pray. Rosa tried to remember some of the words she had heard Reverend Madden use when he prayed in church. Even on a clear day, she could not pray with the fancy words that he used. Mrs. Madden always said God would hear any words she said. Sitting in the dirt, Rosa used her own words to pray.

"Dear God, please help my papá. Please help me. I'm sorry I didn't listen to Mamá. But I don't want Papá to be hurt. Please help me to find him. I trust You to take care of me. Thank You, God. Amen."

Rosa stood up and continued her way along the fence. She no longer noticed the barbs, even though they were still tearing up her hands. One step at a time, she kept going. When she stumbled over a broken fence post, Rosa knew she was getting close to the north end of the pasture.

"Rosa! Is that you?"

Rosa held up the lantern in the direction of the voice. "Papá?"

"Rosa! Over here! Just listen to my voice and keep coming toward me. I see your light."

When she reached Papá, Rosa fell into his arms, sobbing. "I was worried, Papá. I didn't want you to get hurt."

Papá hugged her tightly, then held her shoulders as he looked at her face. "Does Mamá know where you are?"

Rosa shook her head.

"Did you leave the house without telling her?"

Rosa nodded. "I had to, Papá. I had to find you."

Papá held Rosa's bleeding hands. With a handkerchief he tried to wipe the blood away, but the cuts were already full of dirt.

Papá shook his head. "Rosa, you did a dangerous thing. You could have died. You still might die, or your hands could become infected."

"But Papá—"

Once again Papá held Rosa close. "We will talk about this later," he said. "Right now we must find a safe place to wait out the storm."

"I know a place!" Rosa exclaimed. "There's a hut. Rafaél and Juan used to play there. No one lives in it."

"Oh, yes," Papá said. "I remember. It's not too far from here."

"Let's go."

"Rosa, I want you to get on my back. I will carry you."

"I can walk!"

"Rosa, you will obey. I will carry you. You will hold the lantern." Papá stooped down for Rosa to climb on his back.

Papá stumbled once and almost fell. Rosa held on tight and

lifted the lantern high. Once the wind blew out the flame in the lantern, and they had to stop and light it again. This time it took six matches. By the time they reached the abandoned adobe hut, both of them were coughing heavily. Rosa slid off of her father's back, and they both sank to the ground. Some dirt had blown into the hut, but at least they were out of the wind.

"Get as comfortable as you can, Rosa," Papá said. "We will be here for a few hours."

"I'm comfortable as long as I am with you, Papá."

For a long time they sat silently side by side, listening to the storm rage while the lantern glowed at their feet. Finally Papá spoke.

"I'm sorry that the last big storm damaged your school."

"Thank you."

"The workers on the ranch say that the whole building will be torn down."

Rosa looked up in alarm. "Can't they just fix the roof?"

Papá shook his head sadly. "The damage is too great. It would be too hard to make the building safe."

"Where will we go to school? What do the workers say about that?"

Papá shrugged. "Nothing. I hear nothing about that."

"The school board must have a plan," Rosa said.

"I suppose so. I hope so. I know how much you love to go to school."

"Papá, I love learning! The building doesn't matter. I would go to school in this adobe hut if I could learn new things every day."

Papá smiled. "I admire your attitude. You are determined to get an education, aren't you?"

"Yes, I am!"

"What if they don't have a plan for a new school?" Papá asked.

Rosa sighed. "I hate to think about that. But Mrs. Madden says that I must trust God to take care of me. He will help me get the education I want."

"I hope so, Rosita, I hope so."

"Papá?"

"Yes, Rosa?"

"What about the new government project? Is it going to help save the farmland?"

"That is my dream. But we won't know until we try. The scientists from the government say that we can recover the soil when the drought ends. If we do a better job of taking care of the soil, we can farm again."

"And grass will grow for the cattle on the range?"

Papá nodded. "Yes, if the drought ends, grass will grow again."

"You must keep your hope in God, Papá."

Papá smiled. "You are becoming quite a preacher."

"No, Papá," Rosa said, shaking her head. "Mrs. Madden says that everyone can believe, not just the pastor. You must trust God to help you save the soil."

After awhile, Rosa fell asleep with her head on Papá's shoulder and her jacket pulled up around her face to keep the dust out of her nose and mouth. When Papá woke her, the air was quiet. She rubbed her eyes and tried to waken.

"Is it over, Papá?"

"Yes, Rosita, the dust storm has passed. In fact, the night has passed. It is almost morning."

"We've been here all night?"

"Yes, Rosita. When the storm stopped, it was very late. I decided we would be safer to stay the night here."

"Mamá will be worried," Rosa said, "especially because I disobeyed her."

"You will have to apologize for that, hija. For now, let's concentrate on getting home."

Dawn broke just as they finished digging their way out of the adobe hut. It was covered in dust, but the door had been only partially blocked because of the direction the wind had blown during the night. The morning air was still full of dust and looked hazy, but at least they could see where they were going. Rosa hung on to Papá as they walked alongside the fence. Sometimes, though, they could not see the fence because it was buried in dirt. With each step, they sank in the soft dirt. Their progress was slow. Sometimes they had to catch each other as they started to fall.

They passed a plow that Tío had left in the pasture, but they could barely see the top of it. This was the worst storm that Rosa could remember, even worse than the storm that had piled dirt on the school's roof. Rosa wondered if Mr. Garcia had made it home the night before, or if his car would be one of the cars buried in dirt along the road.

"What about the cattle, Papá?" Rosa asked as she looked at the buried plow.

Papá shook his head. "If the dirt has buried the fence, I'm sure we have lost some of the animals, as well. We hardly have any left because we can't feed them. We'll just have to wait and see when we can get out on the range."

Just then, Rosa spotted the house.

"Papá, look! The house is buried up to the windows! Even the front door is buried!"

"Hurry, Rosa, hurry!" Papá began to take longer strides, but the piles of dirt were too deep to run. Rosa did her best to keep up.

CHAPTER 13

Digging Out

Rosa and Papá scrambled up the front steps, which were covered with a drift of dirt. It was as if a blizzard had blown through and buried the house in snow, only it was brown, warm snow. Their steps stirred up the dust once again, and they covered their faces the best they could. Still they coughed and choked on the dirt they breathed in.

Rosa pounded on the front door. "Mamá! Tía! Are you all right?"

No answer came.

"Papá, what are we going to do?"

"We will dig them out, Rosita."

Dirt had drifted up the front door past the handle. Papá began to push dirt around with his hands, looking for the doorknob on the front door.

Rosa's shoes were full of dirt and so heavy that she had to try hard to lift her feet to move around. At first she clomped around, trying not to let her shoes slow her down. The shoes got heavier and heavier. Finally she just pulled off her shoes and clambered around the outside of the house in her stocking feet. Her socks would never be white again after all this dirt, but the important thing was to find her family.

The sun had risen fully by this time, making it easier to see what they were doing. Still, the mounds of dirt were overwhelming.

The first-floor windows were just as bad as the door. Dirt piled so high that no one could see out. Rosa tried to climb a pile of dirt under one window, but she soon sank into its softness. Flailing her arms, she tried to keep from sinking farther as she called for her father. Papá came right away, grabbed her hand, and pulled hard. Rosa flew out of the dirt pile, sputtering and coughing, her face brown with grime. She got back on her feet and brushed dirt out of her mouth.

"Mamá! Tía! Tío!" Rosa called again.

No answer.

"Rafaél! Juan! Can anybody hear us?"

No answer.

Rosa and Papá ran around the house looking for a way to get in. Dirt also blocked the back door.

Papá and Rosa stood side by side, breathing heavily but not speaking or calling out.

"Listen, Papá," Rosa said, "I hear the baby crying."

Papá listened quietly. "I do, too. And your tía is coughing."

"Tía Natalia is going to be very sick from this storm," Rosa said sadly.

"But at least we know they are breathing," Papá said. "If Natalia and Isabella are all right, then I am sure the others are, as well."

"So what can we do?" Rosa asked again.

"We need shovels. They are in the barn."

"I'll get them!" Rosa volunteered.

Papá glanced at the land between the house and the barn. The buildings were not far apart, but the path was deep under dirt.

"No," Papá said, "I will go. You stay here and keep trying to call your brothers."

Papá's voice was firm. Rosa obeyed. She turned back to the house and called out for anyone to hear her, even Isabella. When she glanced toward the barn, she saw that Papá was having a hard time getting through the dirt to the barn. He was not even halfway there. Rosa ran from window to window, calling and calling.

"Rafaél, Juan!" Rosa kept calling.

Finally, outside the kitchen window, she heard a knock. She knew right away that it was her brother Juan, because he loved to tap out messages in Morse code and make people try to guess what he was saying.

"Juan, can you hear me?"

Juan tapped back *y-e-s.*

"Is everyone okay?"

Y-e-s.

"Go to the front door! Papá has gone to get shovels to dig with."

Rosa dashed around to the front of the house.

"Papá, they hear me. They're all right!" she screamed as she ran.

But where was Papá? He was nowhere in sight. The barn doors were still closed.

"Papá!" Rosa screamed. "Papá!"

Crawling through piles of dirt, Rosa moved slowly toward the barn, straining to see through the haze. Papá had fallen, but he stood up now. He was not close to the barn at all.

"I'm coming back," he called to Rosa.

"What about the shovels?"

Papá shook his head. "We'll have to do without them. I can't get to the barn, and the doors are buried, just like the house."

"I can hear Juan tapping," Rosa said. "Everyone is fine."

"Good." When he got to the porch, Papá stopped to catch his breath. "Now all we have to do is get to them."

Side by side, Papá and Rosa began to shove dirt away from the front porch. Handful by handful, the pile was moving. Some of the dirt slid right back into the pile, however. Rosa felt like they were not making any progress.

"We need a bucket or something," Rosa said, "to carry away the dirt."

"We don't have a bucket," Papá reminded her.

"I have a jacket," Rosa said, as she pulled the jacket off her back. "We can fill it with dirt, and I'll carry it away from the house."

"It will be a slow job."

"It will be faster than just digging with our hands."

"All right," Papá agreed.

Rosa tied the sleeves of her jacket together and formed a bowl with the rest. She and Papá scooped dirt into the jacket, and she carried it away. Load after load, they kept moving the dirt. Rosa kept calling to Juan, and he kept knocking on the door in response.

"What is this?" Papá said in surprise, as he reached into the dirt and pulled out something metal. "It looks like Mamá's garden shovel."

Rosa smiled sheepishly. "Yes, that's Mamá's shovel."

Papá grinned at Rosa. "I'm sure your mamá told you to put this shovel away yesterday afternoon."

"Yes, she did, Papá. I know I should be sorry for not obeying, but right now I'm glad I didn't!"

"I am, too!" Papá leaned into the shovel and began throwing dirt over his shoulder at a faster rate. Now they were making real progress.

As they got closer to the door, Rosa heard scraping on the other side.

"Juan is digging, too," Papá said.

"Do you think the house is full of dirt?" Rosa asked.

Papá nodded. "I'm sure it is. I know you helped Mamá stuff rags in the cracks, but the wind was too strong. This was a powerful storm." Papá kept shoveling dirt. Finally, he threw the shovel down and reached for the doorknob. When he pulled it open, Juan fell out through the door.

Rosa couldn't help but laugh. Juan had been leaning on the door when Papá opened it, so now he was sprawled on the front porch with his face full of dirt.

"I think you need a bath, Juan," Papá said, as he helped Juan get up. "Where is your mamá?"

In a few seconds the rest of the family was at the front door. Rafaél had been trying to get out the back door while Juan worked on the front door. Tío was juggling his fussing baby daughter. Everyone hugged everyone else—and then hugged them again. Rosa took Isabella from Tío's arms and kissed her face over and over. Juan raced out to find the animals, taking Mamá's shovel with him. Papá told the story of how he and Rosa spent the night in the old adobe hut.

"Well," Papá said, "I am glad to see that everyone is all right."

After hugging Rosa, Mamá looked sternly at her daughter. "Rosa Margarita Sanchez, you disobeyed me. I told you it was too dangerous to try to look for your papá."

Rosa looked at her dirty socks. "Yes, Mamá. I'm sorry. I know it was foolish."

"Imagine how frightened I was when I discovered you were gone!"

"Yes, Mamá. I'm sorry."

Papá shook his finger at Rosa. "Next time you listen to your mamá."

"Yes, Papá."

Papá looked at Mamá. "Our Rosita had enough sense to bring a lantern and matches. Without the light, we might not have found shelter for the night. So we are all well and safe. But we still have a lot of work to do!"

The floor of the big room was covered in dirt nearly a foot deep. The furniture was just as bad. Rosa walked through the house with Mamá and Papá and saw that every room in the house was filthy. It would take them days to get all this dirt out of the house, maybe even weeks. And then the wind would just blow it back in again, a little at a time.

"We must have half of Oklahoma in our house," Rosa lamented. "Maybe we should just plant a crop right here in the kitchen."

Papá smiled. "We'll make the best of it. Remember, we have hope!"

Now Rosa smiled. "Yes, Papá, we have hope."

Tía Natalia began to cough. Rosa ran and pulled a dishrag from a drawer in the kitchen, then rinsed it out with cold water. When she returned to the living room, Tío had one arm around Natalia and held Isabella in the other. The baby was fussing and wiggling. Rosa put the rag on Tía's face and looked around. There was no place for Tía to sit down and rest. Every chair was filthy. Tía coughed so hard that Rosa was afraid her lungs were going to come up.

"Let me take the baby," Rosa said, as she lifted Isabella out of Tío's arm.

Mamá made an announcement. "The first room we will clean

out is Natalia's room. She must go to bed as soon as possible."

"I'll do it!" Rosa volunteered. She handed Isabella to her mother, and the little girl wailed. Rosa knew she had a lot to make up for in Mamá's eyes. "But what should I do with all the dirt?"

"Throw it out the window," Rafaél suggested. "When we get the inside cleaned up, then we'll worry about the outside."

Rosa scurried into the kitchen for a bucket and a broom, then dashed up the stairs to Tío and Tía's room. Downstairs, her brothers began moving furniture outside so the floors could be cleaned thoroughly. Rosa suspected that some of the furniture was ruined and would never return to the house. She could hear Tía Natalia coughing and Mamá telling Tía to sit in the kitchen to rest.

The sound of Isabella's crying came up the staircase. *She's hungry*, Rosa thought. *Mamá will feed her. Poor Isabella doesn't understand what is happening.* Gradually Isabella settled down.

Over and over, Rosa filled the bucket with dirt and dumped it out the window, adding to the mounds on the ground beneath her. Finally, she had the floor clear enough to mop it. The only clean sheets she could find had holes in them, but that was better than sleeping in dirt, so she put them on the bed. With a damp rag, she wiped out Isabella's basket. She decided right then that Isabella would sleep in her room every night from then on. That way Tía could rest better, and Tío could take care of Tía without waking the baby.

Rosa leaned on her broom, looking out the window and gazing toward town. *Is it like this at everybody's house?* she wondered. *What about Mrs. Madden and Henry? Are they safe?* As soon as she could get out of the yard, she would go find out for herself.

Rosa hated the dust storms more than ever.

CHAPTER 14

Moving On

Rosa and her family were up most of the night cleaning rooms in the house so they could use them. Tía cried herself to sleep because she felt too sick to get up and help. Isabella settled down in Rosa's arms and finally went to sleep. Isabella had a bigger basket now, and Rosa laid her in the basket in a corner of the kitchen. Then she helped Mamá take all the dishes out of the cupboards and wash them one at a time. Before they could put the dishes away again, they had to wipe off all the shelves. Towels and sheets and curtains and tablecloths were blackened. Everything in the house had to be washed before the family could use it again.

The Sanchez family was not alone. The whole town spent days digging out. In fact, people across several states suffered the same way Rosa's family did. Families swept every floor. Women washed every black curtain, every black towel or tablecloth. Ruined furniture piled up at the town dump. Men searched for farm equipment and animals buried in the dust. Dirt in the engines ruined cars. Dirt in the attics made ceilings fall in.

The storm at the end of March had done enormous damage. This latest storm, in the middle of April, was the worst ever. It blew the hope out of many people. Only a fool would try to grow a crop that year. Too much wind, not enough water—farming and ranching were a hard way to make a living. For many families, the April storm known as Black Sunday was the last straw.

A few days after the storm, Rosa walked into town to see how Mrs. Madden and little Henry were.

"Hope, hope," Henry said when he saw her coming. He was out in the yard with his mother. Relief rushed through Rosa. They were both all right. Mrs. Madden was beating the dirt out of the rugs that covered the floor in her house. The rugs hung heavily over a clothesline, and Mrs. Madden used a long stick to beat at them. Her face and hands were already black with the dirt that flew out of the rugs.

Rosa smiled at Henry. "Yes, Henry, hope." But she did not feel very hopeful. She lifted her eyes to Mrs. Madden.

Mrs. Madden put down her stick and tried to wipe some of the dirt off her face with her sleeve. She only managed to smear it around.

"Rosa, I'm glad to see you. Is everyone in your family all right?"
Rosa nodded. "I was worried about you."
"We're fine. Just dirty like everyone else."
"I am so tired of being dirty all the time."
Mrs. Madden nodded. "Yes, we all are."
"Mrs. Madden, why does God keep giving us dust storms when we need rainstorms?"

Mrs. Madden smiled slightly. "I think you know how I'll answer that question."

"Hope. Hope," Henry said.

Mrs. Madden laughed at her little boy. "I hope he still has that kind of hope when he's a little older," she said. "But Henry has it right. We hope in God."

"And He gives us what we need when we need it," Rosa said, finishing the thought the way she knew Mrs. Madden would.

"It is not for us to understand God's ways."

"I would like to understand them just a little bit," Rosa said. "Papá says that more people are going to give up on farming and ranching and go to California."

Mrs. Madden nodded. "Probably."

Rosa was silent for a moment, thinking. "Maybe someone from town will find Téodoro in California and tell him to write us a letter."

"That's a very good idea."

"Can I help you clean the rugs?" Rosa asked.

"Thank you for offering, Rosa, but I'm pretty sure there's plenty of work to be done at your house, as well."

Rosa nodded. "Yes, but we have a big family to help."

"Reverend Madden helps when he can," Mrs. Madden said. "Right now he is visiting someone from the church who is ill with dust pneumonia."

"That's very bad, isn't it?" Rosa asked, thinking of Tía Natalia.

"Yes, it is, Rosa." Mrs. Madden swung at one of the rugs. Rosa stepped back, but still the dust flew at her.

"My tía Natalia is very sick. She can hardly breathe. I help take care of Isabella so she can rest."

"I'll pray for her to get better soon." Mrs. Madden took another swing.

"I wish I could do something to make her better."

"You can pray for her, too, Rosa."

Rosa remembered how she prayed to find her father on Black Sunday and then she found him.

"Mama hit," Henry said, pulling on Rosa's dress.

"I'll play with Henry for a while so he doesn't get in your way."

"Thank you, Rosa. When we get all this cleaned up, we'll have to get back to our lessons."

"I'd like that." Rosa took Henry by the hand and led him away from the rugs.

"Did you hear what the ranchers are saying?" Papá asked Tío about the latest news while they leaned on a fence looking at an empty field. Rosa had a book to read and sat in the shade of a tree.

"What are you talking about?" Tío asked.

"The editor of the newspaper has started a club."

"You know that I do not read the English newspaper," Tío said gruffly. "I don't have time for a silly club."

"This is not a silly club," Papá answered. "It's called the Last Man's Club."

"The Last Man's Club? What is he talking about?"

"He says that the drought has made us all look at the hole. He wants us to look at the doughnut. The drought has not hurt us as badly as it has other parts of the country."

"The drought is hurting us now. Natalia and Carmen have no vegetables to put up for the winter. We have no crop to sell. We have to sell off the cattle before they die, but they are so thin that they are worth very little."

Rosa watched her uncle's face as he spoke. Never before had he looked so worried and discouraged.

"Yes, yes, that's all true," Papá agreed. "But in some places, all those things happened a long time ago. We are just now catching up."

"This is one race I would rather lose."

"You are looking at the hole," Papá said. "To join the Last Man's Club, you take a pledge to stay to the end of the drought. You promise that nothing but extreme illness will make you leave the land."

"This editor asks a great deal. How can we make such a promise? If we cannot earn enough money to feed our families, we may have no choice but to leave."

Leave! Rosa did not want to leave! What about her lessons with Mrs. Madden? What about going to a good school? And she would miss Henry very much.

Papá shrugged. "Men are signing up. Who knows? If the government project works, perhaps there is hope for the land."

"I would like to believe that," Tío said. "My question is, can we last long enough to find out?"

Rosa liked it better when Tío believed the rain would come soon.

California became the talk of the town. The mild weather in California meant long growing seasons. Farmers had several crops to harvest each year—all kinds of fruits and vegetables. Workers moved from one crop to the next, with their children working beside them in the field to earn even more money for the family. Rosa sat on the stairs one morning while Isabella was napping and listened to Papá and Tío talk about it.

"The Delgados are going," Tío said. "They say many Mexicans work in California. Their children are old enough to help them pick."

"The Furmans are also leaving," Papá said.

Rosa's ears perked up. Sally Furman was in her class at school.

"This is just the beginning," Tío said. "I hear a lot of people talking about California. They are trying to decide if they should go."

"They wonder if it is really better than here," Papá said.

"Anything is better than here," Tío said.

"We must keep up our hope," Papá said.

Tío shook his head. "No, Pedro, hope is almost out. How can we survive here?"

"How can we survive anywhere else?"

"We could pick fruit in California," Tío suggested.

Rosa gasped. California? She did not want to move to California to pick fruit. She wanted to go back to school in September. How could she go to school if Mamá and Papá expected her to pick fruit in the hot sun all day long?

"I am not sure everything we hear about California is true," Papá said. "I'm sure people in California have problems, too."

"Nothing is worse than this drought and these dust storms," Tío said. "We should think about California."

Isabella squawked in her basket, and Rosa scampered up the stairs to get her before she woke Tía with her cries.

Even when the wind stopped blowing and the house was clean, Tía Natalia did not get better. Mamá asked her friends about medicine to help Tía get well. Señora Hernandez said to rub skunk grease on Tía's chest. She knew a man who trapped skunks and saved the fat. He would not charge very much for Mamá to buy some. Perhaps he would trade skunk grease for some eggs.

Rosa wrinkled her face at the idea of skunk grease. But if it would make Tía better, maybe they should try it.

Señorita Cruz told Mamá to put a drop of turpentine in sugar and give it to Tía. This would help clear out her throat so she could breathe better. Mamá did try that idea, but Tía did not get better. She only coughed harder.

Señora Garcia suggested a mixture of kerosene and lard. If Mamá would put the mixture on Tía's throat, it might help. Mamá tried that idea, too, but Tía said the smell made her feel even more sick. Her fever went higher.

Mamá took care of Tía, and Rosa took care of Isabella. Tía never came downstairs anymore. Mamá took food up to her, and Tío tried to get her to eat. Sometimes Tío or Mamá stayed up all night with Tía, putting a little bit of food or water on a spoon and trying to get it in her mouth. But she was too tired from coughing to eat and was growing thin.

Rosa was sitting in the shade on the side of the house with Isabella one day when her mother flew out the back door. She ran to Rosa and snatched Isabella from her arms.

"Mamá, what is it?" Rosa sensed panic in her mother's movements.

"It's Natalia. Run, Rosa! Run and get the doctor."

Rosa was on her feet in an instant. Mamá never called for the doctor, because they had no money to pay him. Rosa knew it was serious if Mamá wanted the doctor. She knew right where Dr. Ewbank's office was. Rosa ran as fast as she could. She burst through the door calling for Dr. Ewbank. Three people sat in wooden chairs, waiting to see the doctor themselves. Rosa rushed to the desk where a nurse sat.

"My tía," she said, "I mean, my aunt, she's sick. Very sick. We need the doctor right now."

"The doctor is taking care of other patients right now," the nurse said. "The best thing is to bring your aunt here."

"She's too sick," Rosa insisted. "She's too weak. And Papá never drives the truck anymore. We have no money for gasoline."

"Is she coughing?" the nurse asked.

"She never stops," Rosa said.

"Does she have a fever?"

"It's very high."

"Dust pneumonia," the nurse murmured. "Let me have a word with the doctor. Wait right here."

Rosa waited, her heart pounding the whole time. The few minutes that the nurse was away seemed like hours. When she came back, the nurse had a pencil in her hand.

"Tell me where you live. The doctor will be there in one hour."

"But he must come now!"

"He can't come now, little girl. Your aunt is not the only person with dust pneumonia, especially after that last storm. He will be there as quickly as he can in his car. Now tell me where you live and then go on home."

Rosa swallowed hard as she gave the nurse directions and left the doctor's office. If only he would come right now. Tears slipped from her eyes as she thought of going home and telling Mamá the doctor would not come right away. She hoped that Mamá had not waited too long to call for the doctor.

"Please, God," Rosa said softly, "take care of my tía. Please."

Then she ran home as fast as she could.

CHAPTER 15

Get Out!

Rosa stood in the big room and pressed her face against the dirty window. Where was the doctor? What was taking him so long? Mamá made tea for Tía, but Tía would not sit up and drink it. Tío paced back and forth in their bedroom, wishing he could do something, anything, to make Natalia better. Rosa turned and scooped up Isabella and pressed the baby's face against her own. *Isabella must not know how worried everyone is*, Rosa determined. She began to hum a tune, and Isabella squirmed in her arms to look at her face, smiling.

Juan flew in the front door. "He's here!"

Dr. Ewbank had just turned up the road in his car. Rosa went outside to greet him and led the way to Tía Natalia's bedroom.

Mamá stepped aside as Dr. Ewbank laid his hand on Tía's forehead. "She's burning up. This woman is very sick."

Rosa translated the doctor's words into Spanish, and Mamá's Spanish words into English.

"Nothing we do brings the fever down," Mamá said. "I have tried everything I know."

"She'll have to sit up a little so I can listen to her chest," Dr. Ewbank said.

Again Rosa translated, and Mamá and Tío immediately went

to Natalia's side to help her sit up.

Isabella squirmed in Rosa's arms and reached an arm out toward her mother. "Ma–ma–ma–ma–ma."

Rosa stroked the toddler's head. "*Shh*, Isabella. The doctor is going to help your mamá."

The family hardly dared to take a breath while the doctor moved his stethoscope around Natalia's back and chest. When she collapsed into a coughing fit, he stepped back, and Natalia fell back against the pillows.

"How long has she been this sick?" the doctor asked.

Rosa answered without translating. "She was sick last summer, but she was better in the winter. Now she gets worse with every dust storm."

"Your aunt definitely has dust pneumonia," the doctor said. "She needs to be in the hospital."

Rosa translated, and Mamá and Tío spoke rapidly to each other in Spanish. Then Mamá gestured that Rosa should tell the doctor what they'd said.

"They are afraid the hospital is very expensive. We have not had a crop for two years, and the cattle are dying from hunger. How will we pay for the hospital?"

Dr. Ewbank shook his head. "Rosa, make them understand that this is very serious. I can give your aunt some cough syrup so she can rest better. But she needs constant care. She needs to go to the hospital. Four days ago, I examined a baby with dust pneumonia. His parents did not take him to the hospital. Tell your mother that baby died yesterday. I'm sure you know other families who have lost someone to dust pneumonia."

Rosa translated. Tío began to nod in agreement.

"Good," Dr. Ewbank said. "If your uncle will help me carry her to the car, I will take her to the hospital myself."

Tío was already gently lifting Tía off the bed. As he went past Rosa, he paused to kiss his daughter's head.

Isabella pointed and said again, "Ma–ma–ma–ma."

"Your mamá is sick," Tío said, "but she is going to get better."

Rosa held Isabella tightly as she watched through the window. Tío laid Tía in the backseat with her head on his lap. Dr. Ewbank started the engine.

Tío did not come home all night. With no telephone, the family had no word on how Tía was. Isabella called for her mamá and cried herself to sleep in Rosa's bed.

In the morning, Rosa sat out on the front stoop with Isabella, trying to get the child to drink a little bit of milk. When she lifted her eyes and saw Tío walking up the road, Rosa jumped up, grabbed Isabella, and ran to meet him. Tío carried Isabella, and they walked to the house together. Inside, Tío told about what had happened at the hospital.

"They do not have any medicine to cure dust pneumonia," he explained. "But they are bathing her with cool water all the time, every minute, to keep the fever down. The cough syrup helps her rest. And they keep the hospital very clean. People are mopping the dust away all the time so the patients can breathe clean air."

Mamá nodded. "That's what she needs, rest and clean air."

Mamá fixed Tío something to eat, and then he walked back to the hospital. Rosa walked with him as far as the mailbox. When she pulled an envelope out of the box, she gasped and ran to the house as fast as she could.

"Mamá! A letter!" She waved the envelope in the air as she ran.

Mamá came out to the front stoop, where Rosa stopped to catch her breath.

"It's from Téodoro," Rosa said. "After all these months, he wrote us a letter!"

"Go quickly," Mamá said. "Find your papá and brothers."

Rosa dashed to the barn and the henhouse to find everyone. When the family was all together, Mamá opened the envelope and handed it to Rosa to read aloud.

My dear family,

Greetings from California. I miss you all.

I am sorry I left during the night without telling you. I am sure you know that I wanted to go to California. I hitchhiked out here. I did odd jobs to earn food and slept in barns and cellars or out under the stars. The important thing is that I made it to California.

I came here because I wanted to earn money to send to you. I am sorry that I have not been able to send any money. The stories you hear about the fruit are true. Fruit and vegetable farms spread for miles. The first time I saw an orange grove, I thought I was in heaven. Apples, peaches, melons—they have everything here. When the crop is ready, it must be picked within a few weeks so that it does not rot and fall to the ground. Then the fruit is shipped all over the country. The orange someone buys in Texas may be one that I picked.

I have had a few jobs. The truth is that it is hard to get jobs. It is not hard to know where they are. But many more people want to work than there are jobs. For every job, ten people or even a hundred stand in line, hoping to get that job. Since the owners know so many people are looking for work, they keep lowering their wages instead of raising them. Whoever will work the cheapest gets the job.

If you get a job, you get up long before the sun so you can make your quota before the hottest part of the day. On some farms, workers have to pick all day no matter how hot it gets. You work fourteen hours, eat, clean up, and go to bed. Then you get up and do it all over again. I am trying to save money so that I can send some to you, but it is more difficult than I thought it would be.

I feel sorry for the families. I am a man alone, so I do not have to worry about a wife and children. Often the children work just as long as their parents, but because they are not as fast and cannot carry as much, they do not earn as much money. Many families have no place to live. They make shelters out of anything they can find. They use cardboard and scraps of aluminum roofing and old wooden crates. Perhaps they hang a blanket in the doorway for privacy. Mothers with little babies look hopeless. The babies cry because they are hot and hungry and dirty. There is no place to wash.

In between jobs, families have a hard time finding food. One farmer's pea crop froze in a spring freeze and was ruined. I have seen children out in the fields, pulling ruined peas off the vine to eat.

Rosa would be sad to hear that most of the children do not go to school. They work, or they look after younger children while their parents work. In some places, workers can live in government camps. In those places, some of the people try to organize a small school.

Are there jobs? Yes. Enough for everybody? No. If you work hard for one owner, he might hire you again for the next harvest. Or he might recommend you to another owner.

I am going to find a way to send money. I promise. I hope everyone is well. I miss you and love you. If you write to me soon at the address on the envelope, I think I will get your letter.

Téodoro

Rosa looked up from the letter and saw that Mamá was crying and Papá had his arm around her.

"We will write to him," Mamá said through her tears. "All of us, we will all write him a letter. My son will know that we are happy he is safe and that we love him. Get some paper, Rosa."

"Yes, Mamá."

"I am not a good speller," Rafaél said. "I can't write a good letter."

"You will write the best you can," Mamá said sternly. "Your brother will know how hard you tried."

"Yes, Mamá."

Rosa passed out paper and pencils. Then she sat down and thought about what to write to Téodoro.

Dear Téodoro,

You made us all very happy when we read your letter. Mamá cried. But I don't think it was sad crying. It was happy crying. She is glad to know you are all right. I am, too.

The roof of my school caved in. I don't know if they are going to fix it. But Mrs. Madden still gives me lessons when she can. The dust storms have been very bad, even worse than last year.

Papá is excited about a government project to save the soil.
I take care of Isabella a lot.
Please write another letter so Mamá can cry happy tears again.

Love,
Rosa

The night was hot, and Rosa could not sleep. She crept out the back door to sit outside. Even at night, the air was warmer every day. But outside was cooler than inside.

Rosa heard voices and realized that Tío had come home again. He was talking to Mamá and Papá in the kitchen, and she could hear what they said through the open window.

"The doctor says that Natalia must get out of the dust or she will get sick again. And next time she might not get well."

"What are you saying, hermano?" Mamá asked.

"I must take Natalia and Isabella away from here. We cannot stay here while this drought continues."

"You have always been hopeful that we would get rain," Papá said. "Even more hopeful than I have been."

"I know. But I cannot risk Natalia's health for my own dreams. We will go to California, and I will get a job picking fruit."

"You read Téodoro's letter," Papá said. "It's not as easy as it sounds."

"It's the only thing I can do," Tío said. "Lots of Mexicans work in California. They have been picking fruit for a long time."

"That's true," Papá agreed. "But now people are coming from Oklahoma and Kansas and other places where their farms have dried up and blown away. There are too many workers and not enough jobs."

"We cannot stay here," Tío insisted. "Isabella is starting to cough again, as well. I must take care of my family. If the drought breaks, we can come back."

"Hermano," Mamá said, "we came here from Mexico to be together with you."

"Perhaps we should all go to California," Tío suggested.

Rosa held her breath. She did not want to go to California! Didn't Téodoro's letter say that many children did not go to school? She would be twelve on her next birthday. Mamá and Papá would expect her to work.

"The government is stepping in," Papá said. "They are paying farmers in the dust bowl to use soil-conservation methods. It's going to get better."

"Perhaps. But I cannot wait that long. Besides, you do not own the land that you farm. And you are not a citizen of this country. They will pay the owner, not you."

"If they pay the owner and the soil gets better, then I can grow a crop on his land. And I will learn these new methods for myself. Life will be better for all of us." Papá paused, and Rosa pressed her hands together in hope.

"We are a family, Pedro," Tío said. "My sister is your wife. I don't want to split up, but Natalia cannot stay here."

After a long while, Papá said, "I will have to think about it."

CHAPTER 16

Good-Bye, Jalopies

Tía Natalia stayed in the hospital for three weeks. Tío went to visit every day. Sometimes Mamá went with him and took some of Tía's favorite beans. Day by day, Tía was getting better.

Isabella still called for her mamá, especially at night. Rosa hardly went anywhere without Isabella. She held her little cousin on her lap while she read a book outside in the shade. She held Isabella on her hip while she set the table for supper. She kept Isabella close to her while she studied with Mrs. Madden. Isabella snuggled up to Rosa in bed at night. Isabella started to say a few simple words: *down, me, no, go*. Rosa wished Tía could be there to see her daughter changing.

Finally, Tía came home. Isabella clung to Rosa's neck at first, but Rosa put the child in her mother's arms, and Isabella lit up. "Ma–ma–ma–ma–ma–ma."

"Mamá is home!" Tía said, as she squeezed her daughter.

Tía was not coughing any longer, but she was weak. The doctor told Tío that Tía should not travel for a few more weeks. The trip to California would require strength that Tía Natalia did not have yet.

"Take care of her and be patient," the doctor said, "but moving away from here is a good idea."

120

Tío was not the only one with the idea of moving to California. It seemed to Rosa that every week another family from town packed up and left. Some families were Mexican, and some were white. The drought was hurting everyone: landowners and workers, townspeople and farmers.

Men and boys stuck their heads under hoods to fix cars that were not running. Some people had cars but did not plan to move. They sold these cars at high prices. Families paid all the money they had for a vehicle without knowing if the car would really run well. If they had no money, they traded their most valuable possessions. Then they loaded up and headed for California.

Whenever she walked to Mrs. Madden's house, Rosa could not help noticing who was packing a car or which house was already empty. One day while she was walking home after her lessons, Rosa saw Sally Furman, the girl who had been in her class. Sally's sad eyes stared out a car window at Rosa. They did not wave to each other, because they were not really friends. But Rosa felt sorry for Sally because her family had given up.

The Furmans' car was packed so full there was hardly any room for Sally and her brothers to sit inside. Outside, a rope around the top of the car tied together pieces of furniture piled high. Once Sally read an essay to the class about the rocking chair that her great-grandfather had made. Her great-grandmother had rocked her grandmother in that chair, and her grandmother rocked Sally's mother, and Sally's mother rocked her children. Someday, Sally wanted to rock her own children in that chair. Now the rocking chair was strapped to the roof of the car with blankets wrapped around it. Rosa was not sure the chair was going to make it all the way to California. Maybe that was one of the reasons Sally looked so sad.

Mrs. Madden showed Rosa an article from a magazine about the migrant workers, people who moved to California to go from farm to farm with each harvest. The article showed pictures of a family who ran out of gas on the highway. Another one had a flat tire and no money to buy a new tire, so they camped in the same spot for five weeks. More pictures showed cars with quilts hanging out the back and pots and pans hanging from a rope wrapped around the car. Travelers strapped suitcases and boxes to running boards on the sides of the car. If they had any food, it hung in burlap bags from a rope tied to the car. Most families on the road took with them only what they would need to camp along the side of the road on the way to California, Oregon, or Washington. They slept on the ground or in the car and cooked over a fire.

"Who took these pictures?" Rosa asked Mrs. Madden.

"A photojournalist named Dorothea Lange. She takes pictures of the migrant workers for the government so people can know what life is really like for them."

Rosa wondered if Dorothea Lange would ever take a picture of Téodoro.

All through the summer, jalopies rolled through the streets of town to the highways heading west. Tía Natalia got stronger. After the Black Sunday storm in April, no more big dust storms blew through north Texas—but because there was no rain, the air still was always clouded with dust. Mamá still spent whole days trying to keep dust out of the house so Tía could breathe clean air. Without more storms, Papá began to be more hopeful that the soil could recover.

Mamá sent Rosa into town with eggs every morning to sell or trade. Today, Rosa was supposed to come home with ten pounds of flour so Mamá could make some tortillas. Rosa hefted the bag in her arms as she left the store. Another jalopy rumbled by with pots clanging and suitcases piled high on top.

Rosa's eyes widened. "Mrs. Briggs?"

The teacher heard Rosa call out and asked her husband to stop the car for a moment.

"Where are you going?" Rosa asked, although she knew the answer.

"I wanted to tell you," Mrs. Briggs said. "The farm my husband works on is like all the others. No crops, no money. We need to find work."

"But you have a job at the school," Rosa said.

Mrs. Briggs shook her head. "The school board doesn't have any money to fix the building, Rosa."

"My papá and my brothers would help fix the hole in the roof," Rosa offered.

"The inspector says the whole building is unsafe, Rosa. You know that."

"Where will we go to school?" Rosa asked, her anxiety rising. "No one tells me."

"I don't know, Rosa. Two members of the school board have already moved away. Even if they find a place for school, with so many families gone, they won't need as many teachers. My contract was not renewed."

"They can't do that!" Rosa exclaimed.

"I'm afraid they can," Mrs. Briggs said quietly. "If they reopen the school, they will give the teaching jobs to women with no husbands to take care of them."

"But you're the best teacher," Rosa insisted. "Don't they want the best teachers?"

Mrs. Briggs shrugged. "I'm glad I ran into you, Rosa. I wanted to give you something." She reached beside her on the seat and lifted a stack of books.

"You're giving me books?" Rosa asked.

"You deserve them more than anyone I know."

Rosa looked at the titles: *Tom Sawyer, Moby Dick, Uncle Tom's Cabin.*

"Thank you, Mrs. Briggs," she said softly.

"I'll miss you, Rosa." The car rolled forward as Mr. Briggs pulled back onto the road.

Tío started talking to people about how he could buy a car. Téodoro had hitchhiked to California, but Tío did not want his family to do that. Even if Rosa's family went to California also, they could not all travel in Papá's truck. Every time Rosa heard Papá and Tío talking about California, her stomach got tight.

One night, Papá announced that the Sanchez family would stay in Texas. Papá was convinced that the government projects for taking care of the soil were going to work, and he wanted to learn about them. Rosa jumped out of her chair and screamed with glee. She could hardly wait to tell Mrs. Madden that the Sanchez family would take their chances with the land for another year.

Tío José still planned to go to California. Papá said he could take the truck if he could make it run again.

"I don't understand this paragraph," Rosa said, pointing to a magazine page. "What do people want the government to do?"

Mrs. Madden was gazing out the kitchen window of her house. Henry was banging on a pot on the floor.

"Mrs. Madden?" Rosa said.

Mrs. Madden turned her head toward Rosa. "I'm sorry, Rosa. I was thinking about something else for a moment. Where were we?"

Rosa asked again about the article, and Mrs. Madden explained it.

"So the government wants people to work together to solve the problems many people have," Rosa summarized.

"That's right, Rosa. The government is going to start programs to put people to work or teach them how to do new jobs. If everybody helps, the whole country will be better off."

Rosa tilted her head and thought for a moment. "That gives me an idea," she said.

Henry banged his pan, and Rosa laughed.

"Henry likes your idea already, but I think you'd better tell me what it is."

"We can't use the school building, and we only have one person left on the school board. It will take a long time for the state to do something about our school, so some of the teachers have left town."

"That's right," Mrs. Madden said. "But I still don't know what your idea is."

"You used to be a teacher," Rosa said. "Before you were married, you were a teacher. Why can't you be a teacher again?"

"Me?"

"Yes, Mrs. Madden. You're a wonderful teacher. Look how much I've learned from you. We could start a new school with the students who are left. You could be the main teacher, and I could be your helper. We could combine grades in one room. I'd help with the younger students. We could have school in your church. Reverend Madden would let us do that if we asked. I'm sure he would. He's such a nice man."

"That's quite a speech, Rosa," Mrs. Madden said quietly.

Rosa did not like the feeling in her stomach one bit. "What's wrong, Mrs. Madden?"

Mrs. Madden reached over and took Rosa's hand. "I'm afraid that I have to move away, as well."

Rosa snatched her hand back. "No! You can't! You're a teacher. You can't go pick fruit in California."

"I'm sorry, Rosa. So many families have left that it's hard for the church to meet expenses. Reverend Madden is no longer getting a salary. If he could find another job, he would stay on as pastor with no salary. But you know there are no jobs here, and we are not rich people."

"You can't leave!"

"My mother is ill, Rosa. I don't know how much longer she will live. Reverend Madden and I have decided that the best thing is to move back to St. Louis and help take care of Mother. It will be good for her to have Henry with her, too. She's only seen him one time."

Rosa choked on a sob. "This can't be happening."

"It's so hard to tell you this." Mrs. Madden started to cry, as well.

Henry hit his pot three times. "Osa hope," he said.

Rosa smiled through her tears. "Oh, Henry, I'll miss you. I don't know if I can keep hoping, though."

Mrs. Madden took her hand again. "Of course you can. You're trusting God, remember? We all take chances no matter what we decide to do. Your uncle is taking a chance on California. Your father is taking a chance on Texas. I'm taking a chance on St. Louis. Take a chance on God, Rosa."

CHAPTER 17

Rosa's Idea

Rosa gave Isabella a pot to bang. Her cousin was younger than Henry Madden, but Rosa thought she would have fun banging. And she did. She banged three times with a wooden spoon, then looked up at Rosa for approval.

"One, two, three," Rosa said. "You're a good banger, Isabella."

The baby banged again.

"You know what, Isabella? When you bang a pot, people stop and listen. Maybe I should bang a pot of my own."

Isabella giggled at the face Rosa made. Rosa continued talking to Isabella. She spent whole days with Isabella now. If she wanted to talk to anyone, it was going to be her baby cousin.

"I'm going to miss Mrs. Madden and Henry. I was hoping you and Henry could grow up to be friends. Henry's favorite word is *hope*. So I can't give up hope. Every time I think of Henry, I'll have hope. And every time I have hope, I'll think of Henry and Mrs. Madden.

"Mrs. Madden told me to take a chance on God. Do you think that's the same as having hope, Isabella? I think maybe it is. I don't want to stop learning, not ever! How can I grow up to be a teacher myself if I stop going to school now? The school board doesn't care. The state board of education doesn't care. At least, that's what

I've heard some grown-ups say. But I care. We are going to have a school in the fall if I have to do it myself!"

Rosa thought about what she was saying while Isabella banged.

"That's right," Rosa said. "I'm going to bang some pots, and we are going to have a school. I'll have to find out how many children are left and what grades they are in. Then we have to find a building to use. I still think Reverend Madden's church is a good idea. They have that big room in the basement. We can get desks from the old school and put them in there. I just have to find out who to ask. When I say good-bye to Mrs. Madden tomorrow, I'm going to ask. Even if the church doesn't have a minister, somebody has to be in charge."

Rosa leaned forward and wiped Isabella's running nose with a handkerchief from her dress pocket. Isabella squawked, but Rosa paid no attention.

"But we still need teachers," Rosa thought out loud. "I could write a letter to the state board of education and ask them to send someone, but that will take too long. I must find teachers here.

"I know!" Rosa jumped up, startling Isabella. The baby stared at her with a face that looked as if she were about to cry. Rosa scooped her up. "It's okay, Isabella. I just had a wonderful idea!"

Rosa ran to find something to write on. She used the back of an envelope and made a list of important things to do.

"Why, Rosa," Mrs. Madden said the next day. "It's a wonderful idea. But it will be a lot of work, and you are not even twelve years old. Are you sure you want to try this?"

"Yes, I'm sure," Rosa answered firmly. "This is not just for me.

It's for all the children."

"Well, all right. I'll write down the name and address of the chairman of the church. I only have a few hours before we have to catch our train, so I won't be able to tell him about you."

"Don't worry," Rosa said. "If I have to, I'll take Isabella with me and let her bang her pot. Then he'll listen."

Mrs. Madden laughed with tears in her eyes. "I'm going to miss you so much, Rosa. You have my new address, right?"

"Yes, it's safe in my secret box," Rosa said. "I'll write you letters all the time."

"And I promise to write back."

Little Henry was dressed in traveling clothes. Rosa picked him up and squeezed him and tickled his belly. Henry shrieked with laughter. Rosa kissed his cheek and said, "I'll miss you, Henry."

"Osa hope. Osa hope."

Rosa laughed. "You have to teach him some new words, Mrs. Madden!"

"I'll be sure to work on it. But I don't want him ever to forget to have hope or to forget about you, Rosa."

Rosa felt a knot in her throat, and it was hard to talk. "Mamá is expecting me for supper. I have to go now."

She hugged them both one last time and then walked home without looking back.

Three days later, Rosa stood in front of the house at the address Mrs. Madden had given her. She wore the dress that Tía Natalia had cut down for her at Christmastime, her best dress. She had combed her hair carefully before she left the house. Today she wanted to look grown-up, so she took out her braids. She put one of Mamá's pretty hair clips on the top of her head and let her thick, black, wavy hair hang loose around her shoulders.

"It's time to bang a pot," Rosa said aloud to herself. She marched up the sidewalk and rapped on the door firmly with her knuckles.

When a middle-aged woman opened the door, Rosa said the words that she had carefully practiced all day yesterday, making sure that her English sounded perfect.

"Good afternoon, Mrs. Pherson. My name is Rosa Sanchez. I am a friend of Reverend and Mrs. Madden. I wonder if I might have a moment of your husband's time."

"Come right in," Mrs. Pherson said.

Rosa stepped just inside the house.

"Have a seat," Mrs. Pherson said as she gestured toward a chair. "I will let my husband know you are here."

When Mrs. Pherson left the room, Rosa realized she had been holding her breath. She let her breath go loudly—then put her hand over her mouth and hoped no one had heard the sound. The clock on the wall ticked steadily, and Rosa kept looking at it every few seconds. It seemed like Mrs. Pherson was gone for quite a long time.

"What can I do for you?" said the deep voice of Mr. Pherson as he entered the living room.

Rosa jumped to her feet. For a few seconds, she could not remember the first words of the next speech she had memorized. Finally, she found her tongue. As she described her idea, her own excitement helped her to know just what to say.

One hour later, Rosa ran home. Number one on the list of important things to do was done. Mr. Pherson would let them use the church for a school if Rosa could find teachers.

The next morning, Rosa was ready to start on number two on the list of important things to do. Tía Natalia was getting better every day. She told Rosa that she could take care of Isabella by herself all day.

"Go have a good time," Tía said to Rosa. She thought Rosa would like to go play. She did not know what Rosa had planned, but Rosa was off down the road, happily humming to herself.

She pulled a list of names out of her dress pocket.

Papá had always said that Señor Hernandez was good with figures, and Rosa knew that he spoke English well. He would be a perfect teacher for mathematics, she decided. His son Miguel would be proud.

Miss Cordray, the second-grade teacher from the old school, said that she would help for as long as she could, even if she did not get paid. She could teach the little children how to read. She was going to get married soon, and she hoped that her children would care about learning as much as Rosa did.

Señora Rodriguez had moved from Mexico and become an American citizen ten years ago. She could teach history and citizenship.

When Mrs. Pherson found out what Rosa's idea was, she asked if she could help. Rosa was happy to say that she needed someone to discuss literature with the older students. Mrs. Pherson had her own library in her home and thought that was a perfect idea.

Mr. Roth was a carpenter, and he agreed to rebuild any furniture that had been ruined in the old building. His daughter Angela had told him that the furniture was falling apart even before the roof fell in.

Rosa spent three full days going around to all the people on her list and telling them about her idea. Some people said it would never work. There was no point in trying, so they did not want to help. But enough people agreed to help that Rosa was sure her idea would work.

The next thing on the list of important things to do was to talk to Mr. Orvid, the only member of the school board who was still in town. Rosa remembered when Mrs. Madden talked to the school board about letting the Mexican children go to school with the white children so they would all get a good education. Mr. Orvid had not been too sure that was a good idea. Rosa was afraid he would not like this idea, either.

"But I have hope," she told herself. "I will take a chance."

Mr. Orvid was a banker who helped many of the ranchers in the area. He was busy helping ranch owners and farm renters figure out how they could have enough money to keep going. Some people he could not help, but others he could. Rosa used a neighbor's telephone and called to make an appointment. Mr. Orvid's secretary did not want to give her an appointment at first. But Rosa would not give up until she had one.

Papá went with Rosa to Mr. Orvid's office. When he found out about Rosa's appointment, he did not want her to go by herself. Rosa was glad to have Papá with her. As she waited in Mr. Orvid's office, her stomach jumped up and down, and she had a hard time taking a deep breath. *I'm not finished banging pots,* she thought. *I have to make a lot of noise with this pot.*

At last Mr. Orvid invited Rosa and Papá to come into his

office, where they sat in black leather chairs that were nicer than anything Rosa had ever seen.

"What can I do for you, Mr. Sanchez?"

Papá gestured toward Rosa. "My hija will speak." Rosa knew Papá was nervous about speaking English. He would not say much, but she was glad to have him there.

"Oh?" Mr. Orvid said, looking at Rosa. "Are you going to translate for your father? He really should learn English, you know."

Rosa sat up straight. "I am not here to translate, Mr. Orvid. I am the one who made this appointment."

Mr. Orvid sat back in his chair behind the desk and laced his fingers together across his stomach. "Is that so? Then what can I do for you?" Rosa thought Mr. Orvid looked like he was going to laugh, but she pressed ahead.

"You are the last member of the school board. I would like very much for you to listen to an idea," Rosa said. "I would like to explain the whole idea. Then I will be happy to answer any questions you have." Rosa hoped she sounded serious and grown-up.

"Please, go ahead," Mr. Orvid said, still looking amused.

A few minutes later, he did not look so amused.

"You are the little girl that Mrs. Madden made such a fuss about, aren't you?" he asked.

Rosa nodded.

"And now you come to me with this preposterous notion that you can organize a school?" Rosa was silent. She did not think the idea was preposterous, and it made her angry that he said that, but she held her tongue.

"I suppose you can do whatever you like for the Mexican children," Mr. Orvid said. "But this will never be a real school, so let's not waste any more of my time."

Rosa stood up. "Mr. Orvid, if you have questions, please ask them. I will answer them. This can be a real school if you will help us. The parents will do whatever it takes to meet the state laws for having a school."

"Well," Mr. Orvid said, still shaking his head, "it still seems far-fetched to me. Can you expect me to take this seriously—a child coming in here saying she can organize a school?"

"I am serious, Mr. Orvid."

"I suppose I can play your little game," Mr. Orvid said. "How about if I agree to think about it and let you know?"

Rosa knew that Mr. Orvid said that just to get her out of his office. He would not think about her idea for a single minute. She felt her face flush with anger. Papá saw the expression on her face. He stood up and put his hand on Rosa's shoulder.

"Mr. Orvid," Papá said, "my Rosita, she is not playing game. She want this. She work hard this. We come back three days, and you give answer."

Rosa could hardly believe her ears. Papá was speaking English, and he was standing up for her to the only person who could make an important decision. She stood up tall and threw her shoulders back.

"I'll see you in three days, Mr. Orvid."

CHAPTER 18

Rosa's School and Papá's Dream

Rosa straightened up the fifth-grade history books and stacked the first-grade reading books in a neat pile. She sharpened pencils and collected papers that students had left on the desks. Rosa was in the seventh grade with three other students. The seventh graders were the oldest students in the school. When they were not studying their own lessons, they helped younger students with theirs.

The first month of school had been a success. Señor Hernandez came in the mornings and made math fun by giving students real items to measure and problems to solve. Miss Cordray came before lunch and worked with younger students learning to read while older students read some of Mrs. Pherson's books. After lunch, Mrs. Pherson came to discuss what the students had read while Señora Rodriguez taught history lessons to the other students.

When students saw the new desks Mr. Roth had built, some of the boys asked if they could learn to build things, so Mr. Roth came with tools twice a week after school to teach them. Parents volunteered to come and help students who were having trouble with a certain subject. Rosa herself decided that all the Mexican children would learn proper English, and all the white children would learn a little Spanish.

School had opened right on time. Mrs. Pherson volunteered to be on the school board and filled in all the forms so that the state of Texas would recognize the school as a real school. Mr. Pherson came down the stairs at the church every few days just to see how things were going and make sure no one caused damage to church property. On Sundays, the church members who still lived in town gathered for church services, even if they did not have a minister. Rosa went as often as she could. Church members were more and more proud to have a school in their building.

Rosa usually stayed behind after school to be sure everything was put away properly and cleaned up. At the end of the fourth week of school, she looked up and saw Papá standing in the doorway of the large basement room.

"I was in town trading eggs for beans," Papá said. "I thought I would walk my Rosita home."

"Thank you, Papá. I will enjoy your company."

Papá gazed around the room. "You have done a big thing, hija. You are helping the whole town. I did not understand how important going to school was. You have helped me know that education is important for everyone. When I saw you work so hard to make a new school, I knew that you had learned how to dream big dreams."

Rosa smiled. Papá had never talked about that day in Mr. Orvid's office, but he had helped Rosa in his own way. He went back with her three days later, and Mr. Orvid did not dare to say no. Then Papá gave some of her chores to Juan so she would have time to organize the school. He even said that Juan had to help take care of Isabella. Juan thought that was a job for a girl, but

Papá insisted. He said that Rosa had a real job to do.

Tío worked on the truck. Dust was everywhere under the hood. He had to take the whole engine apart and clean every piece of it. When he needed money to buy parts, he did odd jobs for people who lived in town. The tires were thin, and the windshield was cracked from rocks thrown up by the storms. Even after Tío's hard work, the engine was noisy, and it choked and sputtered all the time.

Rosa was not at all sure that the truck would get Tío and Tía and Isabella all the way to California. He would have to stop and fix it again and again. In her heart she thought that Tío knew that, too. But he said things would never be perfect, so he had to do the best he could. He and Tía tied their belongings in the back of the truck and made a bed for Isabella on the seat between them.

When the day came for Tío and his family to leave, Rosa stood next to the truck, holding Isabella tight and crying. Téodoro left and only wrote one letter. No one really knew where he was. Now Tío, Tía, and Isabella were leaving. Would she ever see her sweet little cousin again? Tío did not know how to read and write very well, but he promised that he would find someone to help him, and he would send letters all the time. And he would go to the place where Téodoro's letter had come from and try to find him.

Juan and Rafaél walked around and around the truck, inspecting and deciding what they thought. Mamá cried. Every time she wiped her nose and stopped, she just started crying all over again. Papá stood with his hands in his pockets, looking somber, and did not speak very much. Isabella did not understand what was happening and wanted Rosa to climb into the truck with her.

With Tía and Isabella in the truck waiting, Tío shook Papá's hand.

"I hope Natalia will be healthy in California," Papá said.

"And I hope your dream of renewing the land comes true," Tío said. "When the drought is over and the land comes back, perhaps we will come home."

Papá nodded without saying anything. Rosa knew Papá did not think Tío would ever come back.

With Mamá crying, they waved good-bye as Tío pulled the rattling truck out onto the road. Mamá turned around and went into the house without speaking.

"*Hijos*," Papá said, "you have chores to do."

"Yes, Papá." Juan and Rafaél headed toward the barn and the henhouse.

"I will miss them so much," Rosa said.

Together Papá and Rosa watched Tío's truck disappear from their sight.

"You have taught me to have hope," Papá said quietly. "I am so proud of you for making your dream come true. Now it is my turn to work hard. I will study at the government project, and I will learn the methods that will bring the land back to us. Someday we will stand out here and look at fields of wheat and pastures of hay. We have many obstacles ahead of us, but I must take this chance to make my dream come true."

Rosa smiled. That was about the longest speech she had ever heard Papá give.

"I'm glad, Papá. Mrs. Madden told me to take a chance on God. And Henry banged his pot and said, 'Hope, hope.'"

Papá nodded. "Perhaps I will go to church with you sometime."

"Papá! I would love that!" Rosa threw her arms around Papá and whispered, "Thank You, God."